Héctor Carré

FEVER

GALICIAN
WAVE THE
WAY
OF FICTION

Published in 2021 by
SMALL STATIONS PRESS
20 Dimitar Manov Street, 1408 Sofia, Bulgaria
You can order books and contact the publisher at
www.smallstations.com

This book was first published in the Galician language as *Febre* by Edicións Xerais de Galicia (Vigo, 2011). The series GALICIAN WAVE: The Way of Fiction exists to showcase the best of Galician young adult fiction in English. More information can be found at www.smallstations.com/wave

Esta obra recibiu unha subvención da Consellería de Cultura e Turismo da Xunta de Galicia
This work received a grant from the Ministry of Culture and Tourism of the Xunta de Galicia

ISBN 978-954-384-127-1

FEVER

Héctor
Carré

Winner of the
Caixa Galicia Foundation Prize
for Young People's Literature

Translated from Galician by
Jonathan Dunne

GALICIAN
WAVE SMALL
STATIONS
PRESS

It had just dawned and a strange warm breeze was blowing. The trees were moving slowly, a hundred arms ready to grab whoever should try to enter their thickness. It was clearly a different day. The atmosphere was as disturbed as life itself, which seemed to have become disjointed forever. It was one of those days that aren't like others. I sometimes think, in moments like that, when the air itself seems lighter, it would be better to stay at home, because if we go out, we may not be able to return, at least to the world we know. But that would be an act of cowardice. You have to go out and confront life, even if everything is turned upside down, as her existence would be that morning.

Back in 1942, everything was in chaos. Shortly after the Spanish Civil War had finished, war had broken out in Europe. The whole world was at war because the Japanese had attacked the Americans in the Pacific. You can't imagine what things were like in those years. I was very young – this was years ago, you understand – and yet it all happened not long ago in my memory. A whole life has gone by, but when you look back on it, a life is like a sigh, an oversight that took you where you least imagined. One day you're at a crossroads; you take one of the roads without knowing you won't be able to go back, without suspecting the road you've walked will disappear forever. You never know if what is in front of you is vulgar or extraordinary. You don't know if what you can see is real or a deceptive appearance. If at that point somebody were to talk about the things we would see change in our lives, we would think they'd completely lost their mind.

The war left behind a state of hunger, death and pain. Pain because of the dead, pain because of the injustice, pain because of the sorrow. When we thought things would change for the better, they took us straight back to the past, to the darkest, blackest period of our history. The situation was sad, desperate, but young people were keen to laugh. We had been through a lot of suffering in our own war, but it was precisely that other war – the war in Europe – that brought a flicker of hope to our region. It was a flicker made of plentiful money, of the desire to live and spend, to enjoy what hadn't been enjoyed in years. We wanted to escape the post-war misery that surrounded us on all sides and to forget all the misfortune we had endured. It was a fever, a wolfram fever.

I told you the day was strange. A warm breeze was blowing at dawn, and that hardly ever happens before the summer arrives, but there it was. That was how it began; after that, everything happened very quickly. I'm going to tell it as I remember it, as if I were watching it on a television screen.

Behind the ridge, there appeared a black shadow. It looked like a mythological animal. It was moving so harmoniously it seemed to have four legs, two arms and two heads. When it stopped, the horse's breath merged in the air with the cloud of sweat surrounding it. Animal and rider were alert. The two heads observed the narrow valley, looking for people on the mountain. But there was nobody to be seen. The rider dug in the spurs and the horse took a leap, throwing back its ears, and started galloping, kicking up tufts of earth and grass as its hooves pummelled the ground.

In the time it takes to close your eyes, the rider crossed the valley and reached the edge of a thick oakwood which covered the descent to the river, narrow and twisted like a humid snake. The rider then pulled on the reins to stop the horse. Being close, although the clothes were not all that feminine, it was obvious the rider was a woman. She wasn't even seventeen, but at that time this was considered old enough to marry. Her name was Carmucha.

For some time now, she had heard about wolfram and the people searching for it on the mountain. Everybody was talking about this. Those who knew what they were saying, and those who didn't. Thirty years later, children still heard their parents tell wolfram stories. 'In the time of wolfram,' they would say, and at those words everybody knew anything could happen. It was like in fairytales: after 'in a kingdom far far away', we all knew anything was possible. When your father was growing up, children would give the mysterious characters people talked about the faces of famous actors, imagining a fantastical world that matched their need for adventure. The stories changed, but at the moment they happened, people talked about them in taverns as if they were adventures from the thousand and one nights, because they were secret and fantastical, because what happened there was extraordinary and incomprehensible. The foreign agents who were involved never explained what really took place. The struggles between English and German spies passed unnoticed beneath a secret blanket of money and corruption. Nobody quite understood why people were prepared to pay so much for the wolfram. That was why the popular fantasy grew in a fabulous broth of adventures, heroes and villains. All kinds of stories were told. Some were absolutely certain, others were exaggerated and still others invented, but they all had the adventurous nature of impossible dreams. The wolfram made some people millionaires and most people mad. The traffic was illegal, but everybody knew it was tolerated. Everybody was acquainted with somebody who knew something secret first-hand. Everybody saw modest men arriving in Noia with their pockets full of money to spend. Carmucha's imagination went wild thinking about those illegal miners. Word had it the mountain was full of people searching for the mineral, chipping away at rocks as settlers do in westerns in search of gold. But this wasn't happening in far-off America, this was happening right next to the summer house her family had in the mountains. That morning, Carmucha had decided to go and see with her own eyes whether what was said was certain. Whether it was true the mountain was full of people around the mine, whether it was true everybody was extracting that black gold in large quantities.

She dismounted, tied the horse to a tree as twisted as a piece of bad advice and entered the wood. The fertile vegetation was bursting all over the place, filling the very stones with life, which were carpeted with moss. The ferns, brambles and gorse gave way to all kinds of weeds, mushrooms and wild creepers. There was not a thimble of earth to be seen. Everything was covered in greenery. Apart from the trees, various formations of rock stood out, rounded like enormous potatoes, with lots of quartz and other metals like tin, which had been taken out of the earth with great effort and discharge of sweat ever since the time of the Romans.

She went over a wall and, having reached the other side, found what she was searching for. In front of her was an expanse of land that looked more like an anthill than a mountain. Groups of modestly dressed people were milling about, chipping away at rocks, carrying bags full of stones, washing the earth in river sieves, talking and sometimes arguing heatedly.

She passed by the people, trying not to draw their attention. She had changed clothes in the country house her family had in the village and wasn't wearing the clothes she normally wore in Noia, but even so, her appearance was still unlike that of the women in those parts. Her English ancestry on the part of her mother and, above all, her untamed character made her unique. However hard she tried to hide it, in that place, it was obvious she belonged to a different social class.

Carmucha gazed hungrily at those farmers who had just become illegal miners, but couldn't locate the face she was looking for. She still wasn't very well known in the free zone, and nobody paid her much attention. Only one girl recognized her immediately. This was Manuela, who was slightly older than her and was wiping the sweat off her forehead with the back of her hand while taking a break from the hard work. Manuela saw her coming like a ferret in pursuit of its prey. That first morning, Carmucha walked among the men and women taken up with their feverish activity as a dream hunter advances in the night, amazed by the shadows of the unknown, but without succumbing to fear.

'What's this then? I'm surprised to see you here!' Carmucha smiled, not knowing what to say. Apparently, she didn't use to talk all that much. 'You're not planning to come and work with us, are you?' Manuela, who was a little on the chubby side, laughed, shaking her body rhythmically. Her rounded face was dirty, but the smile and her vitality gave her a happy, festive expression.

Carmucha shook her head, clinging to her smile timidly before replying.

'I heard your brother was back.'

Manuela nodded effusively and pointed.

'There he is. With Pepiño of Setes and others who used to be miners.'

In effect, Félix was with a group of people who were talking in front of a partially excavated piece of land. He was a strong man, a bit older than they were, and seemed to be mediating between the miners.

'I know he had a pretty rough time, but now they've left him alone, even though he's lost the job he had in the mine. That's why he's here, in the free zone.' Manuela dried the sweat with her hand again and took a step towards her brother, at the same time shouting out to him. 'Félix! Look who's come to pay us a visit!'

Carmucha saw that Félix had recognized her and was smiling affectionately. She made as if to greet him, but at that point the argument between the miners increased in volume, and two men started fighting, attacking each other like wild animals, almost with their teeth. Félix tried to pull them apart, but when some other miners joined the fight, using their tools to hit each other ferociously, he also jumped on top of them, throwing punches with surgical accuracy. He possessed indomitable energy and added a whole lot more violence to the exchange of blows. Carmucha stopped, afraid that Félix might get hurt. Before understanding what was happening, she thought the seed of violence had taken root in all the miners at once, like some kind of instantaneous epidemic, because she suddenly started hearing voices of alarm and shouts of anguish. People were running in all directions, like headless chickens, tripping and falling over in great confusion. In order to go faster, they were downing tools, and even the mineral it had taken them so much effort to extract from the earth. In all the hullabaloo, Carmucha thought she heard some voices warning that the guards were coming. She looked back and saw people running away from the civil guards in their three-cornered hats, which glinted like black steel among the frightened trees.

Having knocked his final opponent down with a cudgel, Félix gestured to Carmucha to get out of there. But she was so afraid she couldn't move. She could see people running, shoving and shouting desperately. She could see Manuela escaping at top speed. She could see Félix, who seemed to be moving away in slow motion, gesturing to her to leave. And she could see the guards coming, but she was paralyzed like a robot which lacks the spark to give life to its mechanical soul. At that point, a shot rang out. It was a sharp bang that echoed, rippling across the mountain, forcing her to run as if she had just received an electric shock on her spine. She heard the explosion as an athlete hears a starting pistol and took to her heels. But she didn't know where the finishing line was. She ran because she was terrified

and stumbled along, not knowing which way to go among all the
miners fleeing the ambush. Then she felt a heavy blow, as if she'd
just collided with a wall, and fell like a sack of potatoes.

She couldn't hear a thing. Just a ringing that increased in
volume. She opened her eyes and saw the world upside down.
She saw the boot of a civil guard stepping next to her head and
followed the leg upwards, searching for the head that governed
that mechanism. Atop the body, she came across the face of a
man who had twisted eyes, was yellow like a sick person's shit
and with a look of disgust was wiping Carmucha's blood off the
butt of a rifle he had just used to whack her. The yellow guard
with the corporal's uniform touched his nose with a rapacious
gesture and spat on the ground. The ringing increased until it
gained hold of her consciousness and Carmucha felt herself
tumbling into a pit of darkness.

The old man interrupts his story and falls silent. There could be a glint of irony in his eyes, but it could also be dejection. He heads towards the bathroom without saying another word.

When he comes back, the girl is still lying on the floor, her feet on top of the coffee table, while watching the television screen. She has this habit of collapsing on the carpet, changing position from time to time, like a pig in the mud.

The old man sits next to her with some difficulty. The sofa is a bit too low – at least for a man who is well into his eighties. The girl is still glued to the screen and pays no attention to the old man's return. He ignores the moving images and looks only at the girl. His tired eyes shine as if some memory had brought back youthful experiences. He looks at her in silence for a good long while before deciding to speak again.

'I reckon it's time I told you…' The girl carries on watching the screen. Only her gesture, lazily lifting a hand, indicates she's heard the old man. 'I've been planning to tell you for some time, but I didn't think you were old enough until now.' The old man talks as if she was paying attention – and he must be a stubborn old thing, because the girl frowns and replies tetchily.

'Grandpa, I'm watching the end of the film.' In effect, the girl's plaintive tone doesn't divert the old man's determination.

'Then turn it off. You'll finish it later.'

'But it's a film. It's at a point where you can't leave it.'

'I know what happens with films, or do you think I'm stupid? I've seen a lot more than you have. When I was young, our old men would tell stories around the hearth, but after that we all started watching films and the stories got lost.' The girl continues ignoring the conversation.

'You'd better pay me attention because I'm not planning to shut up and I won't let you listen to the film.' The girl understands she has no way of twisting the old man's will, clicks her tongue and switches off the set. 'You know something? Those films tell the same things our stories used to tell.' The old man points at the screen. 'The thing is these are in English, instead of the language we used to speak.'

'Yes, I'm sure they're exactly the same.' Irony sweetens the girl's lips. The old man, who picks up on the superior tone the girl is in the habit of using, talks with patience.

'The stories are different, but they always speak about the same things.' The girl listens in silence. Her expression is laden with scepticism. 'I'm going to tell you a story of when I was young. It's like a western, they used to show lots of those. They were the ones I liked best, but they've gone out of fashion. The ones they make now are similar, but take place in other galaxies and there are monsters dripping with saliva, isn't that so?' The girl smiles, thinking her grandfather hasn't a clue about the kind of films that are fashionable nowadays, and changes position, still lying on the floor, making her adolescent hips move like a child going down a slide.

'Why did you say I was old enough?' The old man falls silent, it seems he's thinking about the answer because he's not sure he can tell her the truth.

'Because I'm going to tell the story of a girl who would be about the age you are now.' The girl smiles and, when she speaks, she scrunches up her eyes in a mischievous gesture.

'I bet you don't remember how old I am now, Grandpa.'

'You may be right, but however much you wear those carnivalesque clothes of yours, which make it difficult to see whether you're a horse or a beast, it's obvious you're not a girl anymore, even though you're not fully a woman.' The girl blushes at these words with their sexual connotation.

'Listen up.'

The guards immediately worked out the girl had been in the free zone by chance. It was obvious she didn't belong to the so-called 'searchers', the name given to the illegal miners, so they decided to leave her still unconscious in the house her family had in the village. When Matías – that was her father – received a phone call from the caretaker, he immediately went to fetch her in a taxi and took her to see a doctor in Noia. According to the diagnosis, her condition was not serious, but since she'd received a heavy blow, she needed to sleep and to rest for as long as her body required.

When she finally woke up, covered in sweat as if she had a fever, she saw her father sitting next to her, watching over her uneasy sleep. Matías was in his fifties and, even though the bad life he had endured recently had affected his natural elegance, he maintained a noble, not to say solemn, bearing. He carried on dressing handsomely, in the same clothes he'd been wearing for the last eight years, which were getting more and more worn and dejected, just like him.

When he saw his daughter opening her eyes, he smiled, pushing his anxiety to one side, and took her hand to stroke it tenderly.

'Are you better?'

Carmucha nodded, feeling comforted.

'I saw Félix. He's after the wolfram.' Matías nodded as well, throwing in a condescending gesture which meant something like that's logical since he learned his trade in the mine. Carmucha endeavoured to steer the conversation towards the area her father was trying to avoid. 'He was in prison.'

Matías looked away.

'You shouldn't meet up with him.'

Carmucha was offended by this remark. She clenched her teeth angrily and let go of her father's hand.

'He's our caretakers' son. I messed around with him before I'd even learned to talk. We used to go out on the donkey, he's like a brother to me.'

'But he was always a red.'

The room fell silent, as the whole house full of empty things fell silent, as everybody fell silent, when politics threatened to intervene in the lives of people back then.

'I don't care about politics,' said Carmucha after a brief pause. Matías sighed. That attitude was nothing new in his daughter's behaviour.

'I know, Carmucha. I'm not saying it because of you, but because of me. I'm saying it because of what people might think.'

The blood started to throb in Carmucha's veins. Injustice made her lose her nerve.

'They can think what they like. Mother always said family and friends had to be above everything.' Matías' face grew dark when he heard his wife's name.

'Your mother would agree with me.' Carmucha didn't believe what her father was saying. She gazed at him in silence while the memories took hold of them both, filling that sad room with added sadness. Matías was holding something in his hand. 'What you need is to form your own family.'

Carmucha flung aside the sheets without answering or looking at him. She got up, dressed in her father's pyjamas, and went to the dressing table, deliberately turning her back on him.

'I'm not planning to get married ever.'

Matías hated this rebellious attitude, but limited himself to protesting before his daughter about this habit of using his pyjamas, which he didn't think was appropriate in a young lady. By way of apology, she blew him a kiss in the mirror. Matías smiled. The slightest gesture from his daughter moved him and erased his bad mood. He clenched his fist and went towards her to place what he was holding around her neck. It was a small silver crucifix.

'Do you like it?' He saw her cold gesture in the mirror. Carmucha took off the necklace and placed it on the dressing table.

'Papa, I can't just lower my head. I'm not like Mother.'

He did lower his head, feeling mournful. References to his wife always filled him with sorrow.

'We have to adapt to the circumstances.'

Carmucha fixed him with a look of hatred that hurt like fire.

'So now you want us to pretend to be Catholic? Where's your dignity, Papa?'

'You'll understand as the years go by,' he carried on talking with his head down, a gesture of defeat that repelled his child. 'A woman needs a man to protect her.'

'The way you protected Mother?'

These words hit their target, stabbing Matías' aching heart. He sat on a chair, his mouth full of stones. Carmucha only wanted to discuss the habits that offended her intelligence, but she realized, instead of this, she was causing pain to this defeated man who only a few years earlier had been a happy and strong father. She went to sit on his lap, as sad and desperate as he was. Matías hugged her close and spoke, perhaps more to himself than to his daughter.

'I will look after you even if you don't get married.' Carmucha hugged him as well, recalling forgotten embraces.

'Promise me you won't go to the free zone. It's far too dangerous for a woman.' Carmucha resisted for a moment before replying, gazing at the crucifix on the dressing table.

'All right, Papa,' she said. But she knew an irresistible force inside her was pushing her in another direction.

Carmucha's hands rubbed away, with the insistence of an obsession, at the golden letters of a marble slab on which could be read a name – 'Emilia Finnwater Eastwood' – and two dates – '1897-1937'. She was kneeling in front of the gravestone in Noia's small cemetery. The graveyard looked a bit like a theatre of the beyond, surrounded by houses that were like boxes, from which you could keep an eye on the graves. Many of the stones were hundreds of years old and bore the symbols of guilds that set their tenants apart according to the occupations they'd had while alive. A Romanesque church presided over the scene. Carmucha used that place like a stage set. It was the theatre where she could put on a ritualistic performance whose symbols built a bridge between her and the memory of her mother.

'I have a new pupil. There are twelve now.' She talked quite naturally to the small photographic enamel with Emilia's image, next to which she had deposited a bunch of fresh flowers. 'I sometimes think they don't learn all that much, I suppose I don't know how to teach as well as you did.' She fell silent for a second, as if she could hear the mute stone's response and knew from her voice that the deceased was missing her husband. 'Papa doesn't come as often as I do because it makes him sad, but he remembers you all the time.' As she was pondering silently, she scratched a bit of dust that had fallen on the marble. 'I sometimes get angry with him, it seems he's forgotten all your ideas and doesn't like a woman to have the same rights as a man.' The colour rushed into her cheeks. Betraying her father in front of the photograph struck her as a low thing to do, both because of the betrayal towards him and because of the displeasure it caused her mother. She fell silent so as not to continue digging in the wound.

Having finished the task of cleaning the gravestone, she put the bunch of flowers in their place and sat on the tomb to share with the deceased a few moments of silence in that magical theatre of existence.

Ever since Emily – whom everybody knew as Emilia – had died, Matías had drunk too much, 'too much' being something of an understatement. He hardly had any real friends left, and one of the few he still met up with was Don Severo Mallo, who also liked to party.

'We're Spanish, one of the few serious things you can be in life.'

Don Severo spoke in Spanish, imitating the highfalutin tone of a politician's discourse, but the excess of alcohol coursing down his veins sent his tongue to sleep and made his pronunciation a little hazy. His tense features, as required by the military harangue, suddenly altered, letting out an impetuous guffaw that came straight from the heart. Matías, who was holding onto his arm, also bent double with laughter. A couple of much younger men glugged on a bottle a few feet away, celebrating their own jokes without paying them attention.

'Honestly! That José Antonio Primo de Rivera, what nonsense he comes out with!' Matías grabbed the bottle and took a swig with an emphatic gesture.

'Duke of Rivera, no way! He should be called "Dupe of Rivera"! That's what the wretch deserves.'

They both fell about laughing again and carried on walking sluggishly, stumbling on the stone on the ground, which was exactly the same as that of the houses between which the street ran, very close to the cemetery, beneath the yellow glow of the street lamps. It looked like another stage set where everything had its place, the lights and shadows meticulously arranged to create a harmonious whole. The other partygoers were unaware of this formal balance and helped to cause chaos, breaking the empty bottle on a wall, raising their voices and celebrating the prank as if it had been a great feat. Matías went over to Don

Severo to whisper in his ear, ignoring the hullabaloo their colleagues were making.

'With an ideologist like that, the regime can't go far. Aren't you ashamed to quote such a clown?' Matías was encouraged to talk sincerely because of the effects of the alcohol.

'One gets used to everything. We quote José Antonio because he's dead, and that's a guarantee he won't challenge Franco's power.'

'And you don't talk to persuade the people, you talk to make it clear you're the ones in charge, coming out with the most complete nonsense and doing whatever you feel like, because your power is not based on reason, it is based on force of arms. The more stupid the discourse, the more absolute the power.'

A withered smile clung to Matías' face, and Don Severo didn't want to become serious.

'You're right there, but don't get all tragic. We didn't have such a good time when it was the Republic, did we?'

Matías sighed, trying not to lose his sense of humour.

'Well, that's also true.'

Don Severo sat on the step of a doorway, tired of laughing so much, while the younger lads shouted about who would take the next swig from another bottle they'd taken out of their pockets. At that point, there could be heard the firm footsteps of several uniformed policemen, who arrived with hostile expressions and threatening attitudes. Matías swallowed.

'What's going on here! Be so good as to identify yourselves!' The officer in charge gave the impression he was looking for any excuse to resolve the situation with violence.

'These youngsters are councillors, this is a friend of mine, and I think you know me, right?' Don Severo, who being seated in the shadows hadn't been visible, staggered to his feet and talked while swaying slightly, in a tone that suggested dropping the matter without any more pantomime.

The officer stood to attention and saluted.

'Forgive me, mayor, we received a complaint about the noise, we didn't know...'

Don Severo interrupted him:

'They are the enemies of Spain, barking on every street corner, trying to sully the reputation of good patriots.'

Matías avoided looking at his friend in case he couldn't suppress his guffaws.

'Yes, sir!' The officer stared at the ground, like his companions, wishing they could get the hell out of there.

'We are watching over the nation's interests and deserve a bit of down time, don't you think, officer?' The policeman nodded, getting more and more worried. 'For that very reason, we were just thinking of going a-whoring – if that's all right with you.'

The two councillors looked on in amusement.

'Yes, sir. Please carry on.' All the policemen saluted once more, raising their hands in imitation of the Roman salute, and vanished from view.

'It's wonderful how understanding the police can be in front of the human soul's weaknesses.' Don Severo gestured to the councillors to keep the noise down and continued on his way, holding onto Matías' arm. 'That's why we're fighting, Matías, for a new homeland that understands our highest values and our deepest desires.' He again let out a guffaw and, under the effects of the alcohol, gave his friend a warm embrace. 'That's why you have to join us. I'd like you to be president of the Casino Club.'

Matías received this proposal like a slap. His expression grew imperceptibly colder.

'We live in a dangerous world, Matías. With the Americans on the other side, who knows how the war will end, but with your past...' He paused for a moment during which the two of them exchanged a serious glance. 'You'd do well to heed my advice.'

'But the girl's already giving classes in the Female Section.'

The mayor came out with a vague, sluggish gesture that was like a butterfly struggling against a cold wind.

'You didn't use to mind getting involved in politics.'

Matías breathed out wearily. He knew very well what his friend was referring to.

'But, Severo, you also were in Lerroux's party.'

The mayor's smile was a dry stone which didn't reflect his friend's expression. Matías had lost all trace of happiness, dragged down by the talk and the intake of cheap alcohol.

'It's not the same, Matías.' Severo adopted a slightly patronizing tone, which was adorned with the vehemence of talking while drunk. 'I've always been on the right. But you… You know there are some people who find it difficult to forget… I'm telling you this straight from the heart.'

Matías stopped. The charm of the night was taking off with the wind, merging with some black clouds that threatened rain. Now his past, affixed to his back, was preventing him from breathing normally.

'I don't have the strength.' He looked at Don Severo, as if asking for mercy.

'All right then. That's your business. But don't get all tragic. Come on, come with us, I'll invite you to whichever girl takes your fancy.'

Matías shook his head. He felt a sudden pain that squeezed his throat, as if wanting to strangle him.

'Thanks, but I'm not feeling all that well. Say goodbye to the lads.'

Matías turned and wandered hesitantly down an alleyway. The mayor watched him disappear into the shadows, staggering with lowered head. Having let out a sorrowful sigh, Severo shrugged his shoulders and went to join the councillors, all ready to have a good time in the whorehouse.

In the morning, Carmucha entered the living room with a tray containing coffee and biscuits. The swifts screeched, performing acrobatic hunting moves in front of the gallery. The chestnut dining table which Matías had inherited from his father was solid and dark, but it struck Carmucha as black. Everything in that house struck her as black, darker than it really was, because she had this enormous need to release the frustration that had been growing in her chest for years. She just couldn't find the way to do it.

'When can I go to university, Papa?'

Matías looked up from the newspaper. His eyes revealed the hangover that was piercing his brain.

'What?' Carmucha knew he'd heard her perfectly well and served the breakfast in silence. She sat down to eat with him while waiting for an answer. 'What's all this? You know we don't have money for luxuries.' He talked without looking at her, but she could sense the awkwardness hidden beneath the smile of indifference he was using to shield himself.

'Studying is not a luxury.'

Matías started eating, in the hope he might be able to avoid the matter without making any more remarks, but his daughter was still waiting.

'There's no university here. You're not suggesting going to another town on your own?'

'In Santiago, I could stay with my aunt.' She glanced surreptitiously over the rim of her cup and saw her father, who was increasingly on the defensive, reacting as if he'd just been kicked by a colt.

'Would you be capable of abandoning me just so you can have a degree tomorrow?'

The tick-tock of the wall clock took hold of the room, as if it were the sound of bellows in the inferno. Carmucha looked at him without replying. She seemed incapable of registering what had just been said to her.

'If I were a man, you wouldn't say that.' She stood up and left the room in silence, leaving her father sunk in the half-shadows that threatened to devour him.

Carmucha carried on turning his words over all morning. Those remarks, all remarks like that, made her feel she belonged to a group of second-class creatures. She was fed up of the situation. The blood boiled in her veins.

When it was her turn at the grocer's, a pretty colonial-style store that had lost its splendour because of the scarcity of products on its shelves, Carmucha stepped forwards with the ration book in her hand to take the place another woman had vacated.

'Four packs of fourteen.'

The shopkeeper, a middle-aged man with the look of a tame ox, took the packs and placed them on the counter, a diligent smile dripping from his luxuriant moustache.

'Very good, here's your father's tobacco. Do you have the ration book?'

Carmucha raised her hand, showing the book, but an inner impulse made her beat against the smile on the shopkeeper's face.

'The tobacco's for me,' she said. These words had the same effect as an anarchist manifesto. The five women waiting behind her, accompanied by the odd daughter, observed the scene in horror. The shopkeeper cut off his smile with a knife of disapproval. Carmucha tried to grab the tobacco, but the man's hand got there first, jumping over the packs like a dog guarding its master's house.

'Women have no right to a ration of tobacco,' he said, and immediately he was backed up by several female murmurs.

'Why?'

He hadn't made the law and didn't want to argue with the girl. At that time, it was said that decent women didn't smoke.

In effect, most of them didn't, but he knew that wasn't enough to justify the prohibition. The truth was that Carmucha's question lacked a logical reply. This made him reasonably nervous and he preferred to keep quiet. The women waiting in a line didn't miss a detail and let out hysterical titters because of the girl's provocative attitude. The shopkeeper endeavoured to smile again, but didn't have the strength to stretch his lips.

'I want my tobacco,' said Carmucha, causing the odd client to start complaining. They were automatic complaints, almost inarticulate sounds, a consequence of their natural predisposition – because they were women or because they were Galicians – to defending the established order, whatever it might be, whatever it might determine. Carmucha lacked this instinct.

The shopkeeper was grateful for the gestures of solidarity that arrived from the other side of the front and even dared to crack a joke.

'But why do you want the tobacco if women don't smoke? Are you planning to open a tobacconist's?'

The question had a corresponding effect on the women. Carmucha turned and saw them murmuring and laughing softly.

'I can smoke if I want. Nobody's going to tell me what to do.'

This reply caused widespread hilarity. The guffaws and mocking looks were shared out, passing from the shopkeeper to the mothers and their daughters, etching in Carmucha the need to turn that affirmation into an obvious reality, a reality she would one day be able to throw in those faces deformed by gestures of disgust.

'What a tomboy!' said one client in the ear of the woman in front. Their faces, distorted by the tension and their forced laughter, set Carmucha on edge. 'She pees standing up,' replied the other, talking under her breath, so their daughters wouldn't hear.

Carmucha was fed up of enduring, fed up of thinking the way she was meant to think. For some time now, she had been aware of the death of that world her mother used to talk about, a world in which men and women enjoyed the same rights. Like many good things from her childhood, like her own mother, that world no longer existed. The certainty of its disappearance aggravated the pain at her mother's absence so much she couldn't stand it anymore. She saw those women humiliating themselves, she saw them growing as tense as guitar strings, just because they thought she'd had the nerve to do something without asking for permission, because she'd had the decency to want to do this. Her stomach turned inside out. She didn't want to give them the pleasure of seeing her shout, of losing her temper like an unruly child that is defenceless before its father's authority. She struck out at the packs, sending them flying, and left the shop, looking at the women with a gesture of contempt.

'All right, Grandpa. You've told it now. Can I see the rest of the film?'

'Be quiet and listen. You know perfectly well that's not the end of the story.'

The girl's blood is going to her head and her breathing is slightly disturbed. She's about to succumb to a tantrum.

'But why do I have to listen to a story that doesn't interest me?' Her voice is too loud, impertinent. It's the voice of a spoilt child whose toy has been taken away.

'Because if you don't listen to it, you won't know whether it interests you or not, Marica.' The old man also raises his voice, but with a twist of malice in his expression.

'Don't call me that, it's not my name.' The airs of violence turn now into airs of moaning.

'I'm the only one who calls you the right thing. Your father made a mistake when he put you down in the register. He messed up the letters without realizing, but then he decided he liked it and let it be.'

'You invented that story, Grandpa. Don't you know what Marica means in Spanish?'

'Of course I do, but that has nothing to do with it. In our language, it's a very beautiful name, I've even heard it on TV. I think in Romania or Bulgaria or somewhere like that there are lots of Maricas. There was one – Marica Ungureanu – who ran like the devil.' The girl sighs intensely. She looks at her grandfather with a frown, like a little girl. 'You mustn't be so fanatical, my darling. Your head is closed. You always have a fixed opinion about things. If one day you get to know a series of novels about a child magician, that's all you're interested in, and all the rest is rubbish. Then you take an interest in the history of Egypt, and it's like there's nothing else in the world apart from mummies and pyramids.'

The girl doesn't like listening to the truth when it shows her in a bad light and starts shouting.

'That's because all the rest *is* rubbish. I don't like it. It's rubbish!' The bitterness of despair takes hold of her, making her scream like a seagull lost on an island without wind. The veins in her neck swell as if they were about to burst because in the depths of her soul she knows she's running away from the evidence.

'Of course, like every film that isn't American, like music you don't know, like food you've never tried. Everything is a bunch of rubbish except for the four things you and your school friends enjoy.'

The girl sighs. She knows the old man won't take no for an answer.

'Did they really treat women like that?'

'Yes, they did.'

'That's impossible.'

'Your grandmother lived in that world, and your mother grew up in a world that was pretty similar.'

'All right, Grandpa. We are very lucky to be living nowadays and to have the same rights as men. You've said it now. Can I go back to watching the film?'

'No.'

'But why the hell do you want to tell me this story, Grandpa?'

'Haven't you worked it out?' The old man smiles with a gesture that fills his face with impishness.

When it was time for a walk, and other girls her age got together in groups to show off their finest clothes and to whisper about the boys they bumped into, or would have liked to bump into, Carmucha used to wander aimlessly, dressed very discreetly. Her skirts never had bright flowers and the hems on her dresses were not as obvious as on other girls' dresses. Her clothes, instead of attracting attention, were meant to act as camouflage, because while in the eyes of many she was beautiful, she herself was convinced she was a pebble.

One afternoon, as she was walking down the narrow streets in the centre, staring at the ground, taking care not to step on the lines that separated the paving stones, a group of girls went by, chatting and ignoring her completely. She watched them leave and thought how she wished she could be like them – a normal girl, a girl who didn't worry about unnecessary things – but she knew she couldn't. She lowered her head again and carried on walking.

'Hi, Carmucha!'

When she looked up, she saw a girl smiling pleasantly at her, clinging to her mother's arm like a parrot clinging to the swing in its cage. This girl really was a pebble in all its glory. She stopped to say hello. It was an old school friend by the name of Maribel whose nose was like a brown pepper and whose eyes were tragically close. She'd always got on well with her because she was very friendly. The two were just about to embark on a conversation when her mother grabbed her daughter's arm as if pulling her away from a ditch full of shit. Maribel only had time to quickly say goodbye, her normal, happy expression overshadowed by embarrassment, before being dragged away by her mother, who kept whispering in her ear while glancing over at that strange girl who was the subject of a little too much local gossip.

Carmucha stood still in the middle of the street, offended by this insult she didn't understand and didn't feel she deserved. She was always willing to correct her mistakes, but if someone was wrong in that town, if someone had to change, it wasn't her. She was on the side of right and had no plans to abandon her position.

Her father had asked her to sign up for the Female Section of the Falange, which was the name of the only party allowed under the dictatorship. Ever since, she'd formed part of the teaching body that gave courses of Obligatory Social Service for women between the ages of eighteen and thirty-three. Since the dominant political theme was that men and women were not equal, the women attended classes for just a couple of months while the men did their military service, often in distant cities, or even in Africa. The social-service classes lacked the disciplinary rigour of military service and had no precise programme. In theory, the government was trying to improve the culture of those who attended and to prepare them to carry out different roles in the reconstruction and development of the State. But in reality the only purpose was to prepare them for married life and to fill their heads with political ideas in favour of the regime. Apart from some notions of culture in general, what they studied mainly was cooking, sewing, good manners and the formation of the national spirit. On her chest, Carmucha, who taught grammar, English and world history, wore the badge that marked her as a member of that institution, much against her will. It was a brass piece with the initials 'SS', I don't know whether with the intention of imitating the famous paramilitary organization in Nazi Germany or just by chance. As soon as the class was over, she put the badge in her pocket instead of wearing it all day, as many women did who were proud of that privilege.

Three days after the incident with Maribel, she walked into the classroom and went to clean the board. It was full of sentences of clearly Falangist inspiration. Slogans about victory, about the behaviour of true patriots, and nonsense like that. She took the board rubber and started rubbing, but when she got to a phrase that said, 'The woman only attains human dignity when she serves,' she kept rubbing and rubbing as if wishing to erase all possibility of that sentence ever being written again. She must have spent quite a long time battling against the blackness, because when she realized she'd been cleaning an empty board for a while, she looked at her pupils and observed a scene very similar to the one that had met her eyes in the grocer's. Twenty women sitting at their desks, like rabbits in a farm, watching her maliciously, joining hands and twitching moustaches. They were winking and whispering to each other, as if they were in front of a woman with a dozen monkeys jumping and turning somersaults on her head. Only one girl, a bottle blonde, gave her a sympathetic look, ashamed of the others' behaviour.

Carmucha took a piece of chalk, ready to start the class. Having written the first parts of a verb in English, she broke the chalk, scraping her nails on the board and causing another round of hysterical laughter and mocking whispers. She looked at her pupils. Most of them were older than her and were there simply to tick a box, social service being necessary to secure a post or for any important document – they had absolutely no interest in learning. Carmucha recalled what her mother used to say about school, she recalled her passion for teaching, for getting her pupils to learn things that would help them in the future, and again felt disgust. She knew she was doing something that had no social function, no value.

She chucked the chalk on the desk and left the classroom to the amusement of all the pupils except one.

Once she was outside the building that held the Female Section, she stopped holding back and started walking more and more quickly. She went past a bicycle leaning on a pedal on the pavement and kicked it over. She carried on walking until she got to the cinema, which was in an old house with a colonnade. She went inside to look at the photographs that advertised the film. It was a film with Katharine Hepburn, I can't say which. Like many young women at that time, she felt a great admiration for this artist. She liked her independent style, the free way of living Hepburn stood for and Carmucha dreamed about. She looked at the photos, in awe of the costumes, the cars, the extraordinary world those images portrayed.

'Are you going to give up the classes?' Carmucha turned and discovered the blonde girl who looked at her sympathetically in social service. 'My name's Rebeca, remember?'

Carmucha beamed and nodded. The sympathy they felt was mutual.

'Do you also like films with Katrin Herbun?' Carmucha nodded. 'I need to do social service to get a passport.' She sighed and added in a dreamy tone, 'I'd like to leave for America.'

Carmucha raised her eyebrows in an amused gesture and looked at the photograph of Hepburn.

'The women there are not like us.'

Carmucha's words brought Rebeca back to reality. Her features darkened. She knew she had little chance of ever fulfilling her dream, but since she was a cheerful girl with a wish to seek out the good things in life, she immediately went back to smiling.

'Shall we go for a walk?' Carmucha nodded. 'Then wait for me outside,' said Rebeca.

Before leaving, Carmucha gave her new friend an inquisitive look, but all she got back was an enigmatic gesture. She waited in the colonnade for just a few moments before seeing her emerge, walking quickly. She had one hand hidden inside the old coat she was wearing and gestured to the other to follow. Carmucha obeyed and, once the two of them were walking alongside each other, Rebeca took her hand out of the coat and gave her one of the photographs of Katharine Hepburn she had just stolen from the cinema noticeboard. Carmucha hid it in her clothes and thanked her. She felt this crazy, complete sense of happiness, a childish happiness that lacked all relativity. They spent the whole afternoon walking from one side to the other, as Carmucha used to do, from the park to the quay next to the river, talking non-stop, as if they both had a secret need to share their emotions.

'I have to go now, but I'm free on Mondays. If you like, we can go out some time.' Carmucha accepted enthusiastically and offered to accompany her home. The blonde hesitated. She stared at the ground, trying to resolve the situation without offering too many explanations. 'Don't worry, it's late and I have to run.'

'I like walking quickly,' said Carmucha, quickening her pace and sticking next to her.

They resumed the speed with which they'd left the cinema, but now Rebeca had an inhibited expression Carmucha hadn't seen before and didn't understand.

Night was falling when they reached a crossroads where the street continued forwards, turning into a road that led to the outlying villages. There was another street, a dirt track full of puddles and mud, that led to an area Carmucha wasn't familiar with – her father had told her this was not a suitable place for her; he used to say she shouldn't go there because she might be mistaken for something she wasn't. Carmucha stopped when they reached the crossroads, signalling with a hesitant expression towards the street that led out of town.

'Is it that way?'

Rebeca realized the time had come for her friend to comprehend the situation. She shook her head and glanced in the direction of her own district.

'There's no need to come with me to the door. It's near here.'

The two girls gazed at that district where shadows gathered quickly because of the paucity of the street lighting. Beneath a solitary lamp hanging from a utility pole was a woman who was far more made up than usual. Carmucha suddenly understood the reason why Rebeca had hesitated when she offered to go with her and went as red as a ripe tomato. She was so embarrassed at not having understood earlier that she just wanted to escape.

'All right then, see you. Goodbye.'

Not daring to confront her friend's look, she left in a hurry, her eyes glued to the ground, like the nose of an old dog sniffing a trace of cowardice that gets it away from a herd of wild boar. The prostitute felt hurt, but understood her reaction. Back then, being seen in that place, talking to a woman of ill fame, could have serious consequences for the future of a respectable young lady.

Carmucha hastily opened the door to her house and ran to her bedroom. She closed the door and, once inside, felt safe. She took the photograph of Katharine Hepburn from her clothes and placed it on the bedside table, next to the lamp. She'd walked so quickly she was covered in sweat. She felt afraid, but above all she felt awkward because of her reaction. She was ashamed that she felt comforted by the fact she'd managed to get home without being spotted in that region. Katharine gazed at her from the photograph. This woman lightened her spirits. She was sure the actress, like her mother, would understand her straightaway. But Hepburn's look reminded her of her own mother's disappearance, leaving her alone in that desert where nobody comprehended her. It also reminded her of the cowardly behaviour she'd shown towards that kindred spirit she had only just met. Rebeca had stolen the photograph to give it to her, and she'd repaid her friend by avoiding her like the plague. She felt bad. She felt very alone. She felt like a butterfly in a collection, affixed to a cigar box with a pin.

She left her room in search of her father. As always, the house was dark and had a mournful air. It gave off the sense of abandonment that can be seen in houses when women stop moving the furniture about from time to time. It was full of a threatening silence. She found her father asleep, a book at his feet, in an armchair beside a burning lamp. Next to him was a bottle of cognac that was almost empty like the glass with it. Matías woke up when he heard the creaking floorboards.

'Ah, there you are. Where have you been?'

Carmucha wanted to tell her father what had just happened, but didn't know where to start.

'I went for a walk. Is that cognac?'

'Just a glass.' He gave her a mischievous look, like that of a naughty child, because she got worried if he drank too much.

'Make me some dinner, go on.'

'I brought some eggs from the village. Would you like an omelette?'

Matías nodded and she made as if to head to the kitchen, but before leaving the living room she stopped for a moment and turned to look at him.

'Papa, I'm not going back to the Female Section,' she said, almost without realizing. The words came straight from her heart, without her brain's intervention, but when she heard her voice, she realized she'd taken a firm decision, a decision that made her feel a little better within the constraints of her existence, as if the lid of the cigar box was open and the asphyxiating stench of tobacco could merge with the fresh air of night.

The girl left without waiting for an answer. Matías was petrified, thinking about the consequences of that decision. He quickly grabbed the bottle and poured a large amount of cognac into the glass. He gulped it down, trying to get the bitterness surrounding him to come out of his chest, trapped in the alcohol of his breath, but when he saw he hadn't achieved this, he filled the glass again.

The night was staining the sky black when Carmucha, covered in a headscarf to escape recognition, reached the place where she had taken her leave of Rebeca the day before. This time, there were two prostitutes next to the light. She looked at them, facing up to that dark district like a hole from which drunken, happy miners emerged, and walked quickly into the unknown.

She was full of curiosity, but afraid that she might be attacked or harassed. She soon realized people were wrapped in their own affairs and weren't paying her attention. She wandered through the shadows, spying men who were drinking straight out of labelless bottles and laughing out loud, showing their decayed teeth. She saw an older woman looking for clientele among the oldest, drunkest men, but all she got was a couple of jokes and the odd swig of brandy. A few hungry children were scrabbling around in the rubbish for something to eat. But despite the general misery, she found the atmosphere festive and carefree. She passed in front of several bars full of smoke, out of which came loud voices, laughter and the sound of coplas being played on the most modern gramophones. The houses were low, two or three storeys at the most, and some plots were undeveloped. The empty land was covered in brambles or being used to store things; men made bonfires there, as if it was St John's Eve, but without the need to jump over them.

There was no sign of Rebeca, but Carmucha carried on looking, sure she would find her. In a dark alleyway, she came across a man in an ambiguous position with an effeminate-looking boy. The boy was quite handsome, had wavy hair and a haircut that made him look almost like a girl. She couldn't see the face of the man, who was in the shadows, as his hands ran over the boy and tried to draw him into the darkness. She could only see the outline of his black head, which moved furtively towards the blond boy's back. Carmucha thought she could hear the obscenities the shadow was whispering in the boy's ear and felt utterly confused. At this point, the man's hands advanced across the boy's body and reached his genitals. The boy let out a yelp and, leaping in the air, ran away at top speed, being swallowed up by the shadows. To avoid attracting attention, the man resigned himself to his fate and gave up the idea of going after him. He waited a couple of moments and then came out of the alleyway. Even though he had his hat pulled down to his eyebrows and his collar up, Carmucha could clearly make out the yellow face as he touched his nose with a rapacious gesture and spat on the ground. It was exactly the same gesture she had seen him make on the mountain, after he had knocked her down with the butt of his rifle. The civil guard, dressed in plain clothes, was swallowed up by the darkness.

'What on earth are you doing here?'

Carmucha, still confused, glanced in the direction the voice was coming from. There was Rebeca, in her work clothes, her eyes wide open and a look of surprise etched on her face.

'I came to say sorry.'

At that moment, those happy eyes filled with tears and, even though the mouth broke into an irrepressible smile, Rebeca started crying. She couldn't speak because of the emotion. Her chin trembled and wouldn't let her. She was so moved by the fact a normal woman, what in those days was called a decent young lady, had come to say sorry to her, who had fallen where she had fallen, that it made her feel like a person again.

'I'm not going back to the Female Section, but perhaps I could give classes here, in your district.' Rebeca rushed towards her and gave her a furious hug.

'You're crazy. They won't let you,' said Rebeca after a while, once she had managed to control her emotion and let go of Carmucha.

'The world is upside down, Rebeca. Who's going to care about a crazy woman like me?'

Her friend grabbed her hands and nodded. Her face lit up the whole street, as if it was Pedro Navaja's tooth.

'There are lots of girls who don't know how to read. Can you imagine – I'm one of the cleverest?' She laughed self-depreciatingly. 'Wait here, I'm going to get some money so I can invite you to something.'

Rebeca left without waiting for a reply, and Carmucha felt happy to have dared to go looking for her friend. She was just watching her walk down the muddy street when she caught sight of her father walking towards her, in the company of Don Severo. When they passed next to Rebeca, they both came out with all sorts of compliments before the girl disappeared into a doorway. Carmucha almost doubled over with embarrassment. Matías went up to another prostitute in the vicinity and, sticking his hand wherever he could, rubbed against her with the insistence of a poor man's cloth, lasciviously clutching her buttocks, until the woman pushed him away, back in the direction of Don Severo.

Confused and embarrassed, Carmucha hid in the shadows, her breathing agitated out of fear of being spotted. Matías and Severo passed next to her, laughing and talking like two young lads on the town, ignoring her presence. She watched the men turn a corner and enter the darkness, which swallowed them up like a fish with black jaws.

Some pestilential breath brought her to, as a bottle of smelling salts restores someone who has fainted, when a drunk man came up to her, stroked her and spat at her as he spoke, a few inches from her face.

'I have a black stone and I'm a rich man. I have a stone of wolfram.' Carmucha tried to pull away, but the man, advanced in years, thinking she was a whore, had grabbed her by the waist and wouldn't let her leave. 'How do you fancy spending it with me, pretty girl?'

Carmucha thought about running away, but didn't want to leave the place Rebeca would come back to. She had abandoned her at the first sign of difficulty and didn't want to do it again. She tried to unravel the man's hands, but the old man, smelling like a stray dog, had fingers like forks that clung to her body like hooks being trailed across a net.

'Get away with you! What do you think, the whole sea is made of fish?' Rebeca came back with the money, ready to invite Carmucha, and pushed the old man away like a scarecrow. In view of the prostitute's authority, the drunk staggered off and carried on looking for a woman he wouldn't remember when he woke up, to fritter away his black fortune.

'Come on, come with me.' Rebeca took her arm and led her away.

Meanwhile, Carmucha's father and the mayor were having a few drinks at Rita's, the best brothel in town. It occupied an old summer villa on the outskirts, around which the industry of prostitution had burgeoned as rapidly as the price of wolfram. It was a magnificent modernist building erected at the start of the century, whose luxurious, ornate décor, full of red velvet and golden mouldings, made you forget the miseries and hardships of those times. But the most attractive feature of the house was the women, the most in demand, the ones with the best reputation, and needless to say the most expensive in Noia. Rita, who had known the business ever since she was a girl, because like her mother she had been a whore in the finest houses of Madrid and Barcelona, selected them personally from among the poor wretches that came from everywhere, attracted by the smell of money, or fleeing hunger, bad luck and wartime tragedies.

The rest of the crew of that ship with no fixed route was made up of magma in constant motion – an assortment of miners who'd got lucky, black marketeers and traffickers of various ilks, together with a whole lot of foreigners, spies at the orders of the Third Reich, the British crown or even President Roosevelt of the USA – all seeking to satisfy a yearning that seemed to arise, like the black stuff itself, from the entrails of the earth. After the hunger and sadness the military uprising and war had caused, all people thought about was enjoying life for as long as it lasted.

Matías and Don Severo raised their glasses in a toast, accompanied by two shapely women, and downed them in one go. Don Severo was in a good mood. Having given the girl he'd hired an avaricious kiss, he jumped onto a table.

'Ladies and gentlemen. As mayor of this wonderful town, I should like to introduce you here, at Rita's, the house with the finest reputation in all the region, to the future president of Noia's Casino Club, Don Matías Bermúdez, a man of the future, a guarantor of the New Spain, a loyal servant of the country!'

As he listened to the mayor speak, Matías was greedily licking the girl's cleavage.

When the discourse ended, interrupted only by the odd guffaw, the assembled company broke into applause and acclaimed Matías, who overwhelmed by so much attention stuck his head between the girl's tits, endeavouring to disappear from view.

Carmucha was drinking wine in a third-rate bar where, despite the difference in category, the atmosphere was similar to that in Rita's. There was the same alcoholic happiness, the same convulsive movement, the same amount of smoke, the same vital activity of everybody there. She shared a table with Rebeca, who also proposed a toast. The two of them emptied their glasses, but Carmucha wasn't as happy as the others, she looked somewhat concerned.

'Are all the men here after prostitutes?'

'The ones I know, yes...' Rebeca winked, and the two of them burst out laughing. It wasn't their first drink, and Carmucha looked at her friend in amazement, thinking about all the things she would have liked to ask her if she hadn't been so embarrassed. Rebeca, however, read her thoughts.

'So, what is it you'd like to know?'

'What do men look for in you?'

Rebeca shrugged her shoulders.

'They're off their heads, Carmucha. The wolfram has made them mad. They just want to have a good time while the money lasts.'

'But can you really earn so much with wolfram?'

Rebeca cupped her hand and nodded vigorously.

'I've seen more than one lighting their cigars with banknotes. And now they say the English are buying as well and offering more money than the Germans, can you imagine?'

As she listened to her friend, Carmucha filled their glasses again, her eyes on stalks.

The country house Don Uxío Bermúdez, Matías' father, had had built in the year 1916 possessed something of the Alpine style of summer residences being constructed in elegant places back then. Apart from the main house, which was pretty big, there were stables, sheds and the caretakers' cottage. This was where Manuela and Félix had grown up with their mother, who had taken charge of everything when her husband died prematurely because of a donkey's kick and a bottle of brandy consumed to excess. Mrs Manuela was short in stature and withered for her age as a result of overexposure to the sun and the elements. She was in her early fifties and full of vitality, but unlike her husband she had an active mind and was keen to understand everything that bore any relationship to her.

Mrs Manuela was holding the horse's reins so Carmucha could mount the horse more easily when she saw the girl stick something in her pocket.

'I don't want anything, my girl, there's no need.' She tried to give her back the coins, but Carmucha leaped onto the horse without accepting them.

'Please, Mrs Manuela. You're always giving us much more than we can pay for. I will be offended if you don't take the money.'

The woman accepted this argument because it levelled out the situation between her and the masters.

'Thank you, my girl. Be very careful, everybody's half crazy. And if you see my daughter, tell her to come soon, eh?'

'Don't worry, Mrs Manuela, I'll tell her.' Carmucha tugged gently at the reins and the horse started walking.

She rode towards the free zone, which was the name given to the land close to the mine, but outside the area marked by the administrative concession. This land was criss-crossed by the same veins of mineral being extracted in underground galleries, and people sought them as best as they could, under the open sky, in a more haphazard fashion than in the mine, although sometimes, as Carmucha was about to discover, they used more abrasive techniques.

She got off the horse and tied it to the same tree as last time. She grabbed a bag and the little hoe she'd used as a child from the saddlebags. She'd been given this hoe to muck around in the vegetable garden, playing at helping the grown-ups with their agricultural tasks – she'd always thought the combination of her arms and that little piece of iron made a fabulous tool that was capable of the greatest feats.

When she reached the place where she'd seen people working, she found it deserted. She was afraid she'd gone the wrong way – she didn't always orient herself well on the mountain – but the marks left in the ground and on the rocks by the miners' tools left her in no doubt. She was in the free zone. She gazed at her hoe and suddenly lost confidence in it and in the strength of her arms. But stubbornness was stronger than despair, and she dealt a blow to the rock as hard as she could. The tool bounced on the ground with the selfsame force she had applied and almost hit her in the face. When she recovered from the fright and looked at the place she had just hit, she saw the stone was exactly the same as it had been. It had barely registered a scratch.

'Dynamite! Who goes there? Dynamite!'

Carmucha looked all around, but couldn't see anyone in that broken land full of trees and rocks.

At this point, the earth flew into the air in front of her, as if a part of the planet had suddenly decided to take flight. Immediately after that, she heard a loud detonation and the air gave her a violent shove, lifting her off the ground and depositing her a few yards away. This time, she didn't lose consciousness, but practically the only thing she could see was pulverized earth floating around her. All she could hear was a high-pitched ringing in her ears.

From out of the dust appeared Félix. Carmucha smiled at him, feeling safe, and he, seeing she was alive and in one piece, returned her smile, offering her a hand so she could stand up.

'Are you all right, poor innocent?' Carmucha gave him her hand and got to her feet. Behind Félix appeared some other miners who, like him, had taken shelter, waiting for the dynamite to go off. 'May we know what the hell you're doing here?' He gestured vigorously at her to get her to explain herself, since she seemed to be in a daze because of the explosion.

'I came for the wolfram.'

Félix glanced at Pepiño of Setes and the other miners in their group, who were watching on, bent double with laughter.

'That's the last thing we need. Are you off your head? Can't you see this is no work for a girl?'

Félix took a step backwards and looked her up and down. He ran his eyes over this new woman's silhouette with respectful admiration.

'But... I see you're quite the young lady! And pretty too, even though you're bleeding!'

Carmucha ignored the miners' guffaws, but noticed something strange on her nose. She put her hand to her face. She couldn't feel any pain, but when she moved her fingers away, she saw they were covered in blood. Félix offered her a handkerchief.

'Come on, you, let's get you to the doctor.'

Carmucha took the handkerchief and, when Félix left without waiting for her, followed on behind, drying the blood with that cloth that smelled of gunpowder.

Close by was the bar of Roxelio of the priest. It was called that because rumour had it he was the son of the priest of Lousame. His alleged father had died before the war. Some blamed this death on the government of the Popular Front. They said the anti-clerical politics of this left-wing coalition had caused him so much displeasure his big heart couldn't take any more. Others attributed the heart attack to certain sexual exploits the priest insisted on practising deceptively on his most credulous female parishioners, in spite of his advanced years. I don't know which version is true, but I met the priest and I can say he was the spitting image of Roxelio. Roxelio refused to recognize any father, whatever side of the political spectrum he may have been on. He got on well with everybody, including the Civil Guard, whom he had to pay handsomely so they would let him continue with his work. The bar was next to a couple of houses, the whole of which barely merited the name of village. Félix led Carmucha there along a track that ran through the forest, buried in the earth, since being on the north side of the mountain it spent a lot of time in the shade and the land only ever dried out two or three months in the summer. The rest of the year, cow carts carried mud on their wooden wheels and on the animals' hooves, creating a furrow in the ground. The result was a cross between an ant trail and a trench, from which even people's heads didn't show because of the height of the walls.

When they arrived, they tied the horse to the door of the bar and approached the entrance. Carmucha saw some of the men moving about that place had pistols on their waists. When she remarked on this to Félix, he said it was normal, things were very unsettled.

The bar was pretty big for such a miserable village because Roxelio kept extending it so he could attend to more customers. There was a large counter and several tables among which miners, black marketeers and daring villagers bustled about. The stone walls were quite thick and the windows were small, which meant it was always dark inside, even when the sun was high in the sky. The atmosphere appeared calm, but there was a subterranean current that ran beneath the tables, turning that place into a marsh and tensing the activity of the men there, immersed in tobacco smoke. Carmucha followed Félix to an empty table and noticed, like outside, lots of the men were armed. Félix was delighted to turn up with such a handsome woman and dealt out greetings left, right and centre. The two of them sat down. Carmucha watched in intimidation as the men drank, weighed the mineral on Roman scales and carried out transactions with complete impunity. Félix gestured to Roxelio to come and serve them.

'So what then? I hear you're not reds anymore.' Carmucha ignored this remark and continued watching the spectacle going on around her with fascination. 'Apparently you've turned into first-rate Falangists.'

The boy who served them brought a bottle of brandy and two glasses. Félix poured the liquid up to the rim of the glasses and invited her with a gesture of his hand.

'Didn't you say we were going to the doctor?'

'That's right, woman. And here it is.' He pointed at the glass and downed it in one go. 'A wonderful cure. When anybody here suffers a blow, or something happens, he has a couple of glasses of liquor and is as good as new. Drink yours and you'll see how well it goes down.' He stared at her defiantly and Carmucha felt obliged to drink the brandy. She swallowed it down, but couldn't help a gesture of distaste at the end. Félix congratulated her by slapping her on the back.

'How was it?' she asked, panting because of the taste of the alcohol.

'In the war?'

Carmucha nodded, but that wasn't the full extent of her curiosity.

'In the war, and afterwards.'

'Bad, good, bad again. One gets used to everything, Carmucha. In the war, I saw all kinds of stuff. We killed each other with bullets or with our teeth.' He sighed, shrugging his shoulders, and tried to avert the bad memories by having another drink. He looked at the girl watching him with a sweet expression, as if remembering the happy experiences they'd shared in summers they spent together before that senseless war.

'And how is it here?'

'I don't need to go around showing a pistol because people know I won't back down.'

At this moment, a tall, strong man passed next to their table and greeted Félix with a lot of respect.

'Do you earn a great deal?'

Félix smiled.

'More than I spend.'

Félix drank his glass, and she did the same. The camaraderie that had sprung up between them when they were children had not dissipated with the passing of the years. Carmucha took his hands and smiled affectionately.

'What then? Don't you think I have a future in wolfram?'

'Ah, that depends. If you're not careful, you can have a bad time. See that man who's just come in.' Carmucha looked at the miner carrying a bag of mineral. 'In that bag, he has what he and his companions have managed to get out of the mountain.'

The miner sat at one of the tables where there was a black marketeer. The dealer placed the mineral in the dish hanging off his scales and Carmucha got her first sight of wolfram. It looked as black as jet and was as shiny as the material used by jewellers, but it weighed a lot more, even more than lead.

'The official rate for legal transactions is sixteen pesetas a kilo, but that marketeer, called Miguel Botana, will pay forty because the value of the material on the black market doesn't stop going up.' Behind Botana, keeping an eye on everything that was going on, was an armed man. 'The guy with the pistol works for him. He is paid to stop anyone stealing the wolfram or the money, though they might well try to steal both. If you look at the other tables, you'll see there are lots of Botanas. Everybody's buying for Montaña, which is the name of a German company; that's the name they give them, so they don't have to refer openly to the Nazis who are going to overrun Europe with the cannons made with our wolfram.'

Carmucha looked at Félix again.

'I heard the English are buying as well and are paying more.'

'Yes, I heard that too, but I've never seen anybody here. Perhaps in Noia they'll pay more, but you'd have to get the wolfram there without it being stolen.' At a nearby table, a man started shouting and another two jumped on top of him. A fourth immediately joined the fray. They all started punching and kicking each other and throwing things at each other's heads. The others remained on the margins of the conflict, including Félix, who pretended not to hear the terrible racket coming from the table only a couple of feet behind them. 'How is your father?' he asked as a bottle whizzed past Carmucha, who saw the fight getting worse before she could answer. Some men came over, but limited themselves to waiting for the fight to fizzle out of its own accord when the participants' strength gave way.

'Good... well, not really. Can you come outside for a moment?' Carmucha felt awkward on account of the violent spectacle.

Félix left a coin on the table and escorted Carmucha to the exit, putting his body between her and the fray, so she wouldn't get hit by one of the objects the participants were hurling chaotically at each other.

'Well, if you want to come round these parts, you can always join up with the other women. If you have any problems, just say you're a friend of mine and you'll see how people respect you.'

Félix smiled, talking half seriously, half jokingly, because he was convinced Carmucha would never come back. But she turned around and stopped for a moment, in the middle of that battlefield, to address him with great conviction, even though her expression betrayed the fear she felt.

'I don't want to be a miner. I want to be a marketeer.' She turned around again and headed for the door.

'A woman? You must be off your head.' Félix hurried after her.

Rebeca was waiting at the Verdadeiro, the same bar she'd taken Carmucha to the first night her friend had dared to visit the district. During the day, the bar looked different. There was less noise and the atmosphere wasn't so smoky. That afternoon, just a couple of night drunks served as background music, persisting in a vain attempt to persuade each other where they should go for the next drink. With Rebeca, another three women were waiting. Marisol had come from Madrid before the business with the wolfram had started, escaping a marital persecution she had endured in the district of Vallecas. Remedios the Quiet spoke little and was said to be from Valencia or thereabouts. Those two were more or less the same age as Rebeca. The third was known as the Ourensan and would never see forty springs.

'It seems to me the young lady has gone back to the Female Section,' said the Ourensan. She had been distrustful of women from good families ever since, when she was young, pretty and far too naive, a young lady had stolen the young man to whom she had entrusted her honour and pretty much her destiny a little too blindly.

'I'm sure she'll come,' replied Rebeca confidently, though the others began to mutter under their breath, thinking the Ourensan was right.

The blonde, however, kept looking at the door until Carmucha appeared on the threshold, in a hurry and searching for her with her look. Rebeca took this opportunity to boast in front of her colleagues, arching her eyebrows while casting an ironic glance at the biggest expert of them all.

'Forgive me. I went to the free zone and the bus was late.' Carmucha came over to the table, feeling embarrassed at being the centre of attention.

'Don't worry, woman. Here are your pupils.'

The prostitutes looked at her as if she was a strange insect, a wall of distrust still standing between them. The oldest got ahead of the rest.

'What then? You think you'll be able to get something in our heads?'

'Of course,' replied Carmucha. 'Everybody can learn to read.'

Rebeca, who was known for being dreamy, was brimming with satisfaction when she saw her colleagues open-mouthed, confirming what she had already told them.

'Would you like anything?' she asked Carmucha.

'It's just I don't have any money.'

The Ourensan, who was just about the first in everything, was also the first to break the ice. She had been expecting the girl to never come, but if she did, she had been expecting to see her with an arrogant expression on her pretty young lady's face. She was taken aback by the timid, suppliant look of Carmucha, who was ashamed at having made them wait and apologized sincerely. She smiled and patted her on the back, accepting her good will.

'Come on, you. Start talking and don't worry about the money – we whores will pay for once.' These ingenious words turned into the inaugural speech of the new 'Finnwater School for Women in Need' and, like all inaugural speeches, it was followed by a round of applause and pleasant smiles.

The Casino festivities were famous all over the region. Every night, people came from Muros, Padrón and lots of places, but when there was a dance, they came from as far afield as Santiago, Pontevedra and even Coruña. The atmosphere was elegant, but there were also card games with large bets and business bustled from table to table. People remarked on the vicissitudes of war and read the papers, where news favourable to the so-called Axis powers, that is to say the Nazis and Fascists, always took prominence over the rest. That night in May 1942, the Germans had just launched an attack on Crimea. The war continued to look good for Nazi interests and everybody discussed it. Everybody except Carmucha, who stared seriously at the couples turning round and round on the wooden dance floor. Matías and Don Severo came over to her.

'What's this my eyes see? The Casino president's daughter bored at a dance. That's not possible!' said Don Severo, giving Matías a wink. 'Please, young lady, would you be so kind as to grant me this dance?'

Carmucha looked up heavily. Don Severo was holding out his arm together with a satisfied glutton's smile. Her father also looked in a good mood. She got up, but when the mayor tried to put his arm in hers, slipped delicately to one side and walked away. Matías went after her and grabbed her wrist. He talked to her with clenched teeth, trying not to let the others notice the tension.

'Why are you being like this? You should show more respect.'

'I'm here because you told me, Papa. But you can't oblige me to be happy.'

In effect, more than angry or rebellious, what Carmucha was back then was a sad girl. Matías saw the mayor making a gesture as if to say the girl's attitude wasn't important and let go of his prey. She moved among the people, walking languidly and distractedly.

When Matías looked back at Don Severo, he saw him ceremoniously greeting an elegant, tall, dark man with a carefully trimmed moustache and combed back hair. A serious man who hid behind a pleasant smile fifty-four years of an existence devoted exclusively to doing his duty. The mayor accompanied the foreigner to a free table and gestured to Matías to come over.

'Have you met Don Rüdiger? He's the legal representative for Sofindus in the north-west. You know, Sofindus is Reunited Mines, Marion Transports, the naval group... Sofindus is what everybody calls Montaña.'

Matías shook hands with the Nazis' representative and sat at the table, calling a waiter to come over at once.

Carmucha went to lean against the bar. Nearby was a group of foreigners watching her every movement with glazed eyes. One of them, the most daring or just the most drunk, stood up and held out his hand wrapped in a British smile. Since Carmucha didn't feel like messing around, she turned her back on him without any further explanation. But her behaviour got an enthusiastic response from the British, who applauded her as if they were in a variety theatre. To avoid misunderstandings, she moved away without responding to their acclamations.

Matías listened to Don Rüdiger, who spoke perfectly with a strong Teutonic accent.

'The English were never ones for respecting norms, that's why they're trying to make the market crash by spending like crazy. The fact is they're desperate.'

Don Severo nodded.

'And besides they'll never be able to match German steel,' he added as a show of his unconditional support. Don Rüdiger lowered his voice, talking confidentially.

'Our agents say they're even throwing wolfram into the sea.'

The other two shook their heads like startled birds.

'That's absurd, even for a race as peculiar as the British.'

Matías, who knew his late wife's people quite well, looked at the German and waited for an explanation.

'It's not so absurd. They call wolfram tungsten, but apart from the fact they don't know its real name, if you'll forgive the joke, they also don't know how to use it to harden steel as we do. So why waste more money sending a useless mineral all the way to England?'

Don Severo, fawning, but also polite and talkative, nodded and celebrated Mr Montaña's every word.

'And would you be so kind as to reveal that secret to us?'

The German smiled, glancing around. All the tables were full of well dressed men murmuring amid festive laughter and eyeing up their neighbours. There were glints in those eyes that foretold fabulous business deals and terrible obsessions, passing loyalties and hidden betrayals. There were glints that talked of wolfram and gold, games, forbidden luxuries, fever to live at top speed.

'You'll have to forgive my silence, but you'll understand if I knew that secret, I would prefer to wait for the auction to reach a figure that my patriotism and moral scruples couldn't resist.'

The three of them laughed politely.

Carmucha carried on watching the people, staring at their gleaming eyes with an angry expression. All that joy and festive atmosphere provoked in her only anxiety. A handsome young man wearing a Falangist badge came to offer her his arm.

'Would you like to dance?'

Carmucha glanced at the badge and then looked at the young man.

'My feet hurt.'

The Falangist was prepared to insist, so Carmucha walked away, leaving him with his words in his mouth, so he wouldn't have the chance to try again.

She walked away without thinking where she was going, her only intention being to flee the noise and that joy she was unable to share. She ended up in a corridor where the music and racket were muffled by the distance and the building's capricious forms. She felt better here, listening to that party she couldn't join as if through a mute. She carried on moving in search of tranquillity until she heard another muffled sound, but this sound was much closer, behind a half-open door. It was some kind of death rattle. She looked through the door and saw she was in front of the gentlemen's toilets. Inside, a man was lying on the floor. She hesitated for a moment, but then decided to go and help him. She pushed open the door and entered the room, which was tiled to the height of her eyes. The man was in front of an open toilet, which stank like a babe at the breast when it smells bad.

'Can I help you?'

The man rubbed his mouth with a handkerchief and looked at her in confusion. His face was swollen and his eyes were bloodshot like shameful cheeks. Carmucha had seen him before, in the group of British people huddling next to the dance floor, but she didn't recognize him because she hadn't paid him attention. The young man staggered to his feet, swaying inside his expensive suit, beneath hair that was as unkempt as his tie, offering the perfect portrait of a fun-loving gentleman at the age of thirty.

'Colin Faithless Villanueva, at your service.'

Carmucha was about to leave, but changed her mind when she heard the first of the two surnames.

'Are you English?'

'On the part of my father.' He waited for an answer, but Carmucha, who was waiting in turn to learn more details, remained silent. 'I only just got here. Perhaps you could show me around.'

'Around the toilets?'

Colin laughed. He liked the sense of humour displayed by this girl who was gazing at him haughtily. He thought he recognized that humour as British, but it was simply Galician. A gentleman came in to use the toilets and, when he saw Carmucha, gave a leap as if, instead of seeing a girl, he'd found a goblin in the toilet bowl. The situation was far too ambiguous for the Casino's narrow walls. The same gentleman, a regular client at Rita's, would not have been scandalized or even surprised if he had witnessed a much more compromising scene elsewhere, but this was totally out of place. Colin realized it would be better to leave the toilets and, performing an elegant gesture, he accompanied Carmucha to the door.

'Don't think we English are always like that. War gives us fever, alcohol takes it away.'

'Or gives you more fever.'

'Yes, perhaps. The only ones who don't have fever are corpses.'

Carmucha half-closed her eyes, letting herself be led gently along the corridor, heading back to the racket and the dance floor.

'Aren't you ashamed to be here, getting drunk, while your brothers are getting killed for your country?'

The Englishman's face lit up with an ambiguous smile.

'I don't much feel like giving my life for anything, certainly not a country. But there are many ways of fighting,' he said, deliberately planting a seed of mystery in his answer.

Carmucha nodded, feeling relieved, now she'd reached the point she'd wanted to get to since the start of the conversation.

'Are you here to buy wolfram?'

'I'll tell you if you dance with me.'

The girl raced towards the dance floor, trailed by Colin, whose stomach suddenly felt much better. And yet, after multiple attempts and numerous dances, he understood however hard he tried, he wouldn't be able to get closer to her than a friendly dance between two strangers permits. It was getting late and the dance floor was not so full. There was space to dance at ease, following the orchestra, which attacked each piece of music enthusiastically. Seeing he couldn't go into action, the Englishman resigned himself to conversing with his partner.

'How are you enjoying the dance?'

Carmucha looked him in the eyes.

'I'm trying to sell wolfram. Do you know anybody who's interested in buying?'

'I'll buy everything you can lay your hands on.' They continued dancing, but Carmucha suddenly felt as if she wasn't all there. She hadn't been expecting such an immediate, direct answer. She frowned, unwilling to believe it could be so easy. 'It's true, I swear!' said the Englishman. 'I'll give you 150 pesetas a kilo.'

Carmucha was amazed that things could proceed so simply and irradiated happiness. The Englishman realized this was his last chance and pressed her against his body more than the girl was prepared to accept.

'Thanks for the information. I'll see you,' she said and walked away without waiting for the piece to end, leaving him standing on his own in the middle of the dance floor.

Rebeca and her colleagues got permission from the owner, an ex-prostitute, to use the attic of a local house for free as the seat of the Finnwater School for Women in Need. The premises weren't ideal. They were full of junk, had a low ceiling and got leaks whenever it rained. Not to mention the mice, which they preferred to ignore so this adventure they all felt they had a stake in didn't fail at the outset. Between them, they brought broken desks and benches they found lying about. To the teacher's great surprise, the pupils clubbed together to purchase a small board. They were afraid Carmucha was unhappy and would get bored and stop coming. But she didn't have the slightest intention of abandoning the project. What she had was wolfram fever. Ever since she'd spoken to the Englishman, all she had thought about was the 150 pesetas a kilo he'd offered. With that money, which she thought she could earn easily, she was planning to set up a real school. She was planning to do something her mother would be proud of if she could see her from the other world. She carried on attending classes punctually and going through the ABC, teaching them to read and write with great patience, but her mind could only focus on the wolfram. On days it rained a lot, when they had to interrupt their classes to empty the cans where they collected water from the leaks, she fell silent, staring thoughtfully at the dark corners where the mice came and went, reminding her of her father. She thought about discussing the business and the best way to go about it with him.

Carmucha changed the flowers on Emily's grave while Matías stared at the enamel with his wife's image as if praying.

'Papa, you know the English are buying wolfram for 150 pesetas a kilo, while in the free zone they're only paying forty?' She talked without looking at him, polishing the golden letters of the gravestone as if what she was saying had no importance.

'Where do you get all this nonsense?' Matías would never have been able to imagine the sources his daughter drank from. Carmucha, for her part, believed if she didn't give any details, she didn't run the risk of arousing suspicions about her outings.

'Rebeca told me.'

'Rebeca? What Rebeca is that?' Carmucha noticed a faint shadow of concern in her father's eyes, as if he'd immediately associated the name of Rebeca with that of her friend the prostitute.

'I met her at the social service. She was a pupil,' said Carmucha by way of apology.

'A blonde woman?' The concern spread across his features. He wasn't afraid of being discovered, but nor did he want or feel able to talk openly. Before that conversation, they both believed they were immune from suspicion, but Carmucha, ashamed at not having suspected this before, realized her father probably knew Rebeca very well. This thought filled her with indignation. The idea of her father with Rebeca disgusted her.

'Yes, a bottle blonde. Why?' Matías realized he'd made a mistake by asking about Rebeca, so in the absence of a better path, he decided to get out of trouble by making use of the authority parents exerted over their children back then.

'Be careful. Some of those blonde girls...' he hesitated for a moment because he wasn't sure how to talk to his daughter about such things, '… are women of leisure. You understand my only concern is the company you keep.'

'So why don't you do something about improving the company *you* keep?' The girl stared at him defiantly, with that youthful impetus that always caused her to act with a determination close to that of a desperate woman.

'You don't understand. Severo was never a Falangist. We've known each other since we were kids and I can assure you he's not a bad person.' Matías talked in a pleasant tone, full of patience, which parents need sometimes so as not to ruin any chance of communicating with their children.

'If you yourself weren't ashamed, you wouldn't bother giving explanations.' Carmucha rubbed at the gold again. Matías stared at the ground, remembering a conversation he'd had with Emily shortly before she died. It was a conversation he didn't want to bring up with his daughter. 'Papa, you lead your life, but I can't breathe at home.'

Her father lifted his head, happy to be able to escape those memories.

'But you have lots of free time and I allow you to go riding on your own! What more do you want?'

'I want to buy wolfram in the free zone and sell it to the English.'

Matías couldn't help smiling at this affirmation. It sounded like pure madness. He saw her watching him with those round eyes, that precocious seriousness she'd always had, and thought he could again see the little girl he'd carried everywhere in his arms only a few years earlier.

'Are you off your head, my darling? That's no work for a woman.'

But Carmucha wasn't the girl he remembered. She was a woman. Wounded, but a woman, even though he didn't realize.

'Mother would support me.' She didn't say this to have an argument or to embarrass him in front of the tomb. She spoke without any double meanings because she was quite sure what the mother she idolized would have thought.

'Your mother wasn't perfect, Carmucha. She sometimes made mistakes, like everybody, and she spoiled you rotten.'

The girl filled her chest with air, as if about to jump into the water in order to dive to its depths. Rationally, she knew her mother was a person, and therefore not perfect. But Emilia had died when Carmucha was still a girl, and rationality in children takes second place. To defend herself from such great pain, her subconscious had reacted to her mother's death by idealizing her figure and turning her into a kind of angel, a protective and perfect divinity that accompanied her in moments of suffering and solitude. She couldn't bear anybody talking badly about her, especially her father, who was the only possibility she had left to blame somebody for her misfortune. Her eyes were full of contempt. She was ashamed of what her father had just done. She glanced at the gravestone and left, throwing the cleaning things on the ground, as if she really was afraid her mother might have heard those reproaches. Matías sighed painfully and started picking up his daughter's things.

That same afternoon, Carmucha went to the Verdadeiro to meet Rebeca. Anyone who saw them would have thought they were just another two girls, any old two girls having a drink before going to work. Stuck as they were in the middle of that atmosphere, there was little else they could have imagined. The hubbub would have prevented them from hearing what they were saying. Even if they had drawn closer, they would have carried on thinking what deceitful appearances suggested. They would have seen the blonde woman was tense, moving her feet nervously and not knowing what to do with her hands. They would have seen the other woman talking spitefully and thought – correctly, as it happens – they were arguing on account of some man. But they would have had to get closer to see what the sadder of the two was pulling out of her pocket, to learn that it was a photograph. They may even have had to sit next to them to discern Matías' image stamped on the silver dust of the paper and to see how the blonde woman looked down after observing the image. They would then have heard Carmucha's trembling voice in the middle of all that racket.

'Tell me if you know him, Rebeca.'

They would then have seen the blonde woman dying of shame as she looked up from the table to confront her friend's eyes and nodded imperceptibly, before fixing her eyes again on the red squares of the old, polished tablecloth. They would then have noticed the intense look the other woman gave her, but wouldn't have known what she was thinking. They wouldn't have known if she was angry or prepared to do something; they wouldn't have known, if it was really anger hidden behind those blazing eyes, whether her anger was directed towards the man in the photo or her friend; they wouldn't have known if she wanted to do something to the man or, as a better way of punishing him, to herself; in short, they wouldn't have understood that what Carmucha was really annoyed about was the life she felt obliged to live, which was crushing her within its limits.

That evening, there was no dance, but the Casino was busy like always. Matías occupied a table with Don Severo and a smallish gentleman with an insignificant look. He cut a slightly ridiculous figure, but came from a very rich, very right-wing family that held a prominent position in the life and business interests of Noia. He was called Tirín, though his real name was Edelmiro. As often happens in rich families, this wasn't done to make fun of him by giving him a nickname as ridiculous as he was, but because this is what he said he was called when he started talking, and the name stuck.

'This Rommel must be quite something – you should see what he's been doing to the British in Egypt,' he said, peering at his companions over the top of his reading glasses.

'And what about the Battle of the Atlantic? The allies won't even put out to sea,' declared Don Severo, who had financial interests linked to Tirín's family and was happy to play along. Matías, meanwhile, listened to this bravado with a certain amount of scepticism.

'I suppose there's a little propaganda in all of this,' he suggested before the strained gesture of Edelmiro, who remembered Matías' leftist leanings very well and was easily angered by such lukewarm opinions.

'367 allied ships sunk so far this year in the waters of the Atlantic,' he said, lifting up a copy of *La Voz de Galicia*. 'That's data, not propaganda.'

Matías shrugged his shoulders, not wishing to get into an argument.

The dispute would not have continued anyway because at that point a woman dressed as a man entered the hall of the Casino. Matías immediately recognized the suit because it was his. Carmucha was searching for him with her look. By the time their eyes met, the woman dressed as a man was the centre of attention of everybody present. At their table, the silence was like at Mass and Matías' look was that of a man witnessing a sacrilege. In front of the high altar, right in the middle of that community that had assembled to reassert itself, Carmucha was launching a direct attack on good order and social harmony.

The girl smiled.

Matías, having excused himself before his table companions, went to break that smile he considered a mockery. He broke it with a hard, sonorous slap. Carmucha was petrified by this reaction. It was the first time her father had hit her. He'd done it in public in an attempt to erase the affront she had just inflicted on the governing elite. Carmucha offered no resistance when he pulled her out of the room, without any shrill sounds, the way an ox pulls a cart.

'Have you gone mad, or what the hell is the matter?' Matías spoke through clenched teeth so nobody would hear them, but the scandal had already been served. Tirín directed a knowing look at Severo, who lowered his eyes in shame.

'What a butch!' declared that ridiculous man, saying out loud what everybody else was thinking.

Matías dragged his daughter to the door and pushed her into the street. He pulled on her arm so hard she fell to the ground, on paving stones that were wet because of the night dew. The street was quiet. The stars shone in the black sky and people passing by kept to themselves.

When Carmucha endeavoured to stand up, she got such an almighty slap that she fell down again. Matías was out of his mind. He couldn't understand what his daughter had intended, who was looking at him again inexpressively. He lifted her up, stood her on her feet, without getting any reaction. He gave her another slap that turned her head. When she looked back, her nose was bleeding profusely, but she was still as silent as the grave. That was what enraged him more than anything – her silence, her lack of explanation or protest at the hiding she was getting. He shook her, grabbed her by the neck, like a murderer, with bloodshot eyes, without getting a peep out of her. He wanted to say something, to ask for an explanation for that crazy act she had just put on, but his nerves wouldn't let him. He gave her another hard slap with the back of his hand, and was about to deal out another when Carmucha took to her heels.

'Come here! Come back right now if you don't want to end up in a convent!' he shouted, finally recovering his speech.

But she didn't want to hear him. She ran and ran, blinded by tears, crossing the night like an invisible shadow, crossing well paved streets until she reached the limits of the town, where the streets were even darker than the night, but the ground was softer, and hungry children were still looking for something to eat.

She knocked, banging on a door with knuckles scratched by the paving stones outside the Casino, and when the refuge opened, letting out warmth and party lights, she went in before anybody could realize she was a woman. She looked for Rebeca among the girls, but couldn't find her. The men discovered this boy was in fact a woman in disguise and were as taken aback as if they'd seen a ghost. Some of them, accustomed to Rita's surprises, even thought this was a new, highly sophisticated prostitute and tried to take her hand, to stroke her, the drunkest among them to fawn on her as if they were kneading bread. So it was that Carmucha added disgust to bitterness and was about to expire with anxiety when she finally spotted Rebeca coming out of the area of private rooms, accompanied by two men.

'You have to help me,' she said, on the verge of tears.

The old man falls silent. The girl he called Marica looks at him, waiting for him to continue, but the man's mouth remains closed, his gaze more impish than before, perhaps because he knows he's finally captured the girl's attention.

'All that fuss because some broad dressed up as a man?' The girl talks with feigned indifference.

'It was another time. Women dressed as women, men as men. There were only two sexes, and no mixing. Even at school, boys were separated from girls.'

The girl laughs at such eccentricities.

'Are you serious?'

'Absolutely.'

'So what would they think of me?'

'During carnival, they'd think you were a joker; the rest of the year, they'd think you were crazy or a lesbian, which is what they thought of her.' The old man stretches out on the sofa, as if he needed a little rest after recalling all those adventures. The girl looks at him, moving her foot. She seems restless. She looks at him, scratching her arm. She twirls like a reel in front of the old man's silence.

'Grandpa, you don't think I'm a lesbian, do you?'

'Are you not?' The old man comes out with a mischievous grin, but the girl is not amused by his joke.

'Would you mind if you had a lesbian granddaughter?'

'I know it's fashionable to be bisexual these days. I read in the paper you get entangled with each other like dogs, which if they can't find a bitch will jump on any old leg.'

'Grandpa, don't say that!' she shouts again like a baby in the cradle.

'There's nothing wrong with being lesbian. At your age, I wasn't sure about anything, certainly not my sexual orientation –

I didn't even know it existed, the way you do today. But when it comes down to it, with everything you know, you're like us, because you're at an age when you doubt. You want to know who you are. You're desperate to find what you're looking for, without knowing what it is. It was one thing yesterday, and now it's another. In our time, we used to doubt whether we would find a woman, whether she would love us, whether she would prefer somebody else, and in the meantime we got it out of our system any way we could. Today, it's fashionable to doubt, to try here and there, but the fact is a person who doesn't like cheese, however many times he tries it, will still not like it.' The girl is calmed by these explanations, but remains silent, confused by the ironic sexual allusions. 'You would certainly have to be desperate to do what she did, getting dressed up like that.'

'But I don't do it to cause a scandal, I dress like that because I like it.'

'I know your thing is something else. You wear those military trousers hanging off your behind to keep in with the skateboarders who spray walls with letters they can't read. Your style is a bit frivolous, but it's just fashion. You don't dress like a scarecrow to look like a man, but she didn't do it because of fashion.'

'Why did she do it?' the girl dared to ask.

'Out of desperation. She never had any doubts about her sexuality. She dressed as a man because men didn't have to ask for permission to do what they wanted.'

'Are you telling me it wasn't her intention to cause a scandal?'

'It was a threat. Without physical violence, but with a terrible amount of symbolic violence that left her father totally defenceless before her. He didn't know how to face up to that rebelliousness.'

'Parents always say children are rebels.' The girl thinks she's found a card she can use in her arguments with her father.

'That's right, but she had a reason to rebel. She was different. You're not a rebel, you do the same as all the others in your group, you buy the brands sold by your idols. That's called consumerism, not rebelliousness. You protest because you have to take the rubbish down and you leave your dirty plate on the table for someone else to tidy. You don't like responsibility, you prefer to carry on being a babe at the breast until you're thirty, like everybody in your generation. You're not stupid, you're shameless.'

The girl recovers the cynical expression she had at the beginning and goes back to the story to escape the disagreeable turn her grandfather has given the conversation.

'So what did her father do?' she asks.

Matías spent the whole night waiting. As soon as it began to dawn, he got dressed and went to look for her. He scoured the town a hundred times, without finding a trace of his daughter, not daring to ask anybody if they'd seen her or could give him some news as to her whereabouts. The second night, he didn't sleep either. He didn't know whether he should go to the police to report her disappearance, but preferred to cling to the idea that nothing had happened to her, she had run away and was hiding, as a way of punishing him. He carried on waiting all day, he had no appetite and was listless, and when night came, he went to the Casino, in the crazy hope she might just come back, even if she was dressed as a man.

He went to the bar and looked at his pocket watch with a weary expression. Needless to say, Carmucha was nowhere to be seen. Miguel Estévez, a waiter with a lot of experience who'd come from Coruña to work in the Casino because the pay there was very good, came over to him.

'Would you like anything, Don Matías?' The waiter noticed his concern and the bags under his eyes.

'A cognac,' replied Matías, trying to appear calm. 'Listen, Miguel, you don't happen to know whether my daughter's been in today?' The waiter poured the cognac into a large, round-bellied glass.

'No, sir. She hasn't been in today.' He had plenty of time to serve and keep an eye on the customers, but the delicate nature of this affair prevented him from looking up from the counter.

Matías gestured his thanks and focused on the cognac, wondering what he could do to get his daughter back.

'You look terrible. What on earth's up?' Don Severo clapped him on the back, smiling impishly, thinking his appearance was due not to worry, but to some nocturnal outing. Matías hadn't told him about Carmucha's disappearance and, like everybody else, the mayor thought the girl was shut up at home, paying for her misdeeds with some obligatory confinement.

Matías dragged the mayor to a table far too vehemently to keep an appearance of calm.

'Could you lend me some money?'

Severo couldn't understand the serious, almost tragic, look on Matías' face.

'Come now. Is that all it is? I was beginning to think you had a serious problem.' The mayor smiled, relaxed because of the request.

'It's just lately…'

Don Severo interrupted him, refusing to hear any explanation. He didn't want his friend to feel awkward because of a financial matter during that year of plenty.

'You don't have to say anything. It's down to us to set an example, and that's enough. You don't have to worry about money.'

'Thanks a lot, Severo.'

The mayor wrinkled his mouth, determined to make the matter appear less serious, when a young Casino employee came over to the table, carrying an envelope on a tray.

'Don Matías,' the boy offered him the envelope.

The president of the Casino ripped it open, not hiding his concern. Inside the envelope was a perfumed note which said, 'Don't miss the novelties at Rita's.' He folded the piece of paper and put it in a pocket thoughtfully.

'Are there some new whores at Rita's?' The mayor's curiosity got the better of him – he was convinced Matías had been visiting the brothel on his own as well as with him.

'Not that I know of. Have you heard something?' Matías was so worried he didn't even realize what his friend was thinking. 'Forgive me, I have to go out for a while.' He stood up and left, followed by a mocking smile from Don Severo, who had got the wrong end of the stick. He'd mixed all the ingredients –

note, brothel, eye bags, need for money – and come to his own conclusions by adding: girl, dazed man, need to spend what you don't have on business relating to her.

All the details were correct, but the mayor's conclusion, with Matías in some kind of illicit love nest, was completely false because he'd ordered the ingredients in the most logical, perhaps even the most common, way without realizing the girl he had added to the broth was not from Rita's, but was Carmucha, and everything that had to do with her was always closer to being extraordinary than run-of-the-mill.

Matías reached the brothel with his heart beating like a procession of cripples. He'd often gone in there in high spirits, looking to satisfy a yearning that would help him forget his problems. At that moment, the same faces of the girls who normally aroused his fantasies contorted his spirits as if they were stones that had fallen in his stomach. None of them helped to resolve his enigma. What novelties could there be for him at Rita's? He leaned on the counter and gestured to the waiter, putting a thumb to his mouth.

'Rita isn't here, is she?'

The waiter shook his head and served him a drink. Matías wanted to talk to her in case it was Rita who'd sent the note. Then he saw Rebeca. The girl smiled at him as on other occasions, but he didn't know how to react. Rebeca kept looking at him, she even gestured to him to go over, albeit she was with two clients. Matías didn't feel able to go over and ask if she knew anything about his daughter. He stared at the ice cubes in his glass, wondering whether he should pluck up the courage to go and talk to her. Rebeca used this opportunity to gesture to a colleague, who shot out of the lounge.

Matías watched the cubes dissolve in the gin, moving them by swaying his glass. He was lost. He looked up, feeling defenceless, and saw in the middle of the room, walking towards him with a huge grin, a terrible novelty with the clothes and hairstyle of an employee. The girl pushed away the hands of other clients, which kept landing on her like flies on honey. It was Carmucha. He felt the need to release his anguish with a good slap, but was gripped by fear of a scandal.

'What the hell are you doing here?' he asked with a look of hatred.

'And you, Papa?'

Matías thought this was getting out of hand. After what she'd done, after what she was doing, she still had other things to tell him. He was about to lose his temper, but realized nobody was paying them attention. Carmucha came over and leaned her head on his shoulder, like a lover or a daughter. This gesture, despite its double meaning, placated him at once. The physical contact with her banished all the fear he was carrying inside.

'Have you always liked this type of atmosphere, or is it a recent hobby?'

Carmucha caressed him the way she would at home, but hadn't done in public since she was a little girl.

'That's none of your business.'

Matías swallowed some gin to give himself some courage.

'And was it Mother's business?'

Her father moved away a little too abruptly. Some heads turned without conscious awareness, an automatic reaction that accompanies sudden movements in our field of vision.

'Shut your mouth. Don't talk about your mother,' said Matías, while Carmucha smiled at an unknown man who was looking at them.

'Why don't we come to an agreement and avoid a scandal?' The girl came over again and wrapped an arm around him with the same affection she'd always shown, as if it was just the two of them at home and there was nothing untoward.

Matías was indignant, but the only path open to him was the one his daughter was offering. It was either that or carry out the threat of sending her to a convent. This possibility struck him as worse than losing her forever. He looked at her. She was so close that, without glasses, he saw her out of focus, and so dolled up, more than he'd ever seen before, that she looked like one of those strange paintings he'd viewed at an exhibition he'd been to with Emily, when the two of them had visited Paris in the late 1920s, when Carmucha was still very small, before everything had gone to hell. He exhaled bitterness and, placing a hand on her head so she would rest it on his chest, greeting a few acquaintances and feigning a great triumph, when what he'd suffered at the hands of his daughter was a great defeat, he left, full of contradictory feelings.

The dark living room of the family home was the only witness to the terms of the agreement. Only a couple of table lamps were on. The two of them were like statues, still and quiet, having ended the argument that had begun when she was getting changed. Her father could not forgive the scandal she'd caused, nor understand why she'd done it. Carmucha just wanted him to understand she was prepared to do anything so he would let her get involved in the wolfram business. They were silent for a long time, while Matías finished digesting the toad he'd been forced to swallow.

'Tell me why. Why are you doing this to me, Carmucha?'

She sighed as her father had done. The words, caught between doubts and fears, stuck to her thoughts, wouldn't come out of her mouth.

'The world is collapsing, Papa. The world you knew is about to disappear. But my world has sunk already, and I need to lift my head. I want to look at the sky without fear or shame, I want to remember my mother and fight for what she fought for.'

Matías swallowed saliva with a knot in his throat. He was dying to press her against his breast and to tell her that everything was all right, he forgave her and always would forgive her, whatever she did. But he was still terribly displeased by her behaviour and believed he had to punish her by remaining cold and focusing on the commercial details, so she would understand the gravity of what she'd done.

'All right,' he came straight to the point. 'In this business the return is raised thanks to the capital and, since I'm the one putting up the capital, I'll get eighty percent of the profits. Agreed?' Carmucha nodded eagerly at this unjust proposal. 'All the money will pass through my hands and I'll pay your share into a joint account. In exchange, you'll behave properly and will stop making me look ridiculous. Do I have your word?' Carmucha stood up, ready to seal the agreement with a kiss, but her father simply offered her his hand. She shook it, feeling ashamed, and Matías left the room, unable to look at her.

The women were washing the earth with miners' sieves in the river pools. The sun shone that summer as spring nights shine in the hearts of lovers. Carmucha was dying to get started.

She arrived at the river on her horse and saw Manuela drying the sweat on her forehead with the back of her hand, as she was wont to do when working alongside her colleagues. The miner went to greet her as soon as she recognized her. Carmucha dismounted.

It was the month of July and hot, but to her this was a different heat, as the summer was different. It was her first summer as a woman after all the bitterness she had endured during the final years of her childhood.

'Hi! I see you've decided to finally come and work with us!' said Manuela, having a go. Carmucha shook her head and, smiling pleasantly, went to talk to her in private.

'You get paid forty here for the wolfram, am I right?' she asked, taking her by the shoulder.

'Recently we've been getting paid forty-five,' Manuela corrected her with the look of a professional.

'I'll pay you sixty-five. Are you interested?' The words came out of her mouth with such certainty it would have been impossible for anyone to realize her legs were shaking.

Manuela was stunned and couldn't understand. She found it difficult to accept she had just heard a much more favourable proposition than she could have imagined.

'Crikey! Of course I'm interested!' she said, slapping her thigh loudly after a moment's hesitation.

Whether Carmucha had lost her mind or this was just a foretaste of the changes that were coming and Manuela couldn't see, the fact was the deal sounded more than interesting. This was the basis of Carmucha's strategy. She thought if she was going to get involved in that illegal trade, where people were always suspicious and afraid of getting ripped off, her best option was to earn the women's trust. She didn't mind offering almost fifty percent more than the local marketeers because she wasn't planning to sell to the Germans at Montaña, but to the English, on the basis of Colin's offer. The women with Manuela came over, their curiosity piqued by their colleague's words and gestures.

'This is Carmucha, the lady from the big house, some of you know her,' she said by way of introduction.

The women nodded or smiled, all eager to learn the news that lady with a youthful face kept hidden beneath her serious appearance.

She earned their trust and managed through them to buy small quantities of wolfram from the miners in the free zone. She never bought everything, so they would carry on selling to their usual marketeers – she didn't want them ganging up on her because she was paying such high prices. She went from place to place, carrying water in zinc jugs and giving it to people to drink. She seemed to devote herself to this labour of solidarity with the miners out of a maternal instinct, as if she was a voluntary nurse, something that went well with her social condition and class. In this way, she had access to everybody and little by little, without arousing suspicion, she acquired more and more of the mineral, which she paid for with the money her father had given her, always in small amounts. She had some Roman scales in her saddlebags and weighed the wolfram wherever she might be, only making sure she wasn't seen by indiscreet eyes. She kept the mineral in a box hidden in the shed of their country house and spent a month on the mountain, filling her saddlebags bit by bit, working from sunrise to sunset, until she had amassed a hundredweight.

At the beginning of August, Carmucha returned to the Casino, dressed in the way her father liked. Matías smiled with pleasure when he saw her coming in, stepping firmly like a sunny day, and sighed when he remembered her mother. Carmucha was wearing a dress that was tight around the waist and moved in folds that flowed from the waist as if shaken by the wind. It was a suit of her mother's.

She went to sit on a sofa from where she could see the Englishmen's table. Colin wasn't there. She got ready to wait, reading the paper. Her attention was drawn by a headline. Gandhi was threatening the British with a fast unto death if India did not receive her independence from the British Empire.

She was fascinated by this unusual challenge, a challenge that invited them to protect the life of a single man in exchange for losing a country the size of a continent, a challenge that threatened the British with the elimination of their greatest enemy unless they bowed before him. It was surprising, but to her mind it was much more than that. It was the perfect example to show the whole world how the weak, like her, could fight against the strong if they had right on their side.

There weren't any photos in the paper. Just a text describing the pan-Indian congress in Bombay. She imagined Gandhi dressed in his white rags, acclaimed by the crowds, as the news agency said. She imagined that insignificant man bringing a whole empire to its knees with only the force of his words. It was an extraordinary news item. She looked up, having read the whole article, and saw Colin coming in. She put the paper to one side and went to meet him, intercepting him before he could reach his table. When he saw her, he stopped and waited for her.

'Well, well, well! The wolfram lady. To what do I owe the pleasure of your company?' Colin had not forgotten the way she'd left him standing on the day they met and laced his words with plenty of British – or was it Galician? – irony.

'I have wolfram to sell,' said Carmucha, chewing the beats of a racing heart.

The Englishman's expression altered. Irony turned into curiosity. He went to an empty table and sat down with feigned indifference, the same as her, who imitated his behaviour with great naturalness.

'How much exactly?'

Carmucha felt intimidated. It hadn't occurred to her to think the quantity might be relevant.

'About fifty kilos.'

Colin let out a polite, merry guffaw, eyeing her with acres of superiority.

'May I buy you a drink?' he said in English, thinking she wouldn't understand.

'Do you want the wolfram or not?' replied Carmucha without enlightening him. She didn't like being looked at like that, as if she was still in the cradle and adults were cooing over her.

'I thought we were being serious. For a quantity like that, nobody will lift a finger.' The girl fixed him with a stare that hurt, but the Englishman didn't flinch, he just wrinkled his smile.

'The last time we didn't talk about minimum amounts.'

'The last time we didn't talk. I was drunk and you left me standing in the middle of the dance floor like a scarecrow.' Carmucha looked down in shame. 'You must forgive me, but I wasn't sure you were being serious. This is a real business. It's not for you. Why don't you head on home and think about redecorating your room?'

Colin stood up, glad to have got his own back on that lofty girl, but Carmucha grabbed his arm like a fork and stopped him in his tracks.

'Tell me a minimum amount.'

Before replying, Colin observed the hold she had on him with slight amusement and looked into her eyes, where she was waiting, sharp as a knife.

'Half a ton.'

Carmucha let go of his arm as if she were tossing him aside and didn't want to see him again. Colin took his leave very formally and went to sit at the table of the English. Carmucha felt desolate. Five hundred kilos sounded like an impossible amount.

Black as moles, the clouds gathered in the sky. The storm wouldn't take long. The heat was sticky and didn't make it easy to work, but Carmucha had no wish to rest. She had lots of wolfram to gather.

'Is that all…?' She let the last word float in that atmosphere full of noise that hadn't burst yet and got no answer. 'How about Félix? Your mother told me he was here somewhere.'

Manuela shrugged her shoulders. Carmucha closed the bag of wolfram to put it in her saddlebags.

'He'll be here somewhere, but you know what he's like. I haven't seen him for a couple of days,' she said, waving goodbye to a woman who had just sold them half a kilo of material.

They then heard running, the heavy steps of an angry man, the steps of frightened women running to escape the wolf, the steps of an uneasy horse. Carmucha understood a patrol was coming and slapped her horse's haunch. The animal galloped off and disappeared among the trees. The women escaped uphill, leaving their tools behind so they could get away more quickly. Manuela advanced next to Carmucha, who ran with the bag of wolfram in her hand. The civil guards had reached the river.

'Get out of here! We don't want illegal miners in this zone!' shouted the guard in charge.

Carmucha hid behind a tree and heard a shot. She recognized the yellow guard, who was shooting into the air without looking where he was shooting, holding the reins of a nervous horse. She watched the women still running uphill and heard another detonation. Manuela fell as if that explosion had passed right through her. Carmucha saw Yellow holstering his pistol, letting a colleague shoot again, before pointing to the wounded miner. Manuela didn't move, she just moaned in a broken, muffled voice. The other women approached, not daring to touch her. The guards also ran over to where she was.

It was as if a performance had suddenly come to an end, as if tragedy had deviated from the usual script and that farce of guards pursuing women had been cancelled until the extent of the misfortune could be ascertained. Carmucha remained behind the trees, unable to believe what she was seeing. Her tears fell on dry earth, as if the storm had finally unleashed all the suffering she carried inside. The miners clustered around Manuela, carrying in dirty hands the shouts they didn't want to let out, clinging to their ripped clothing, like martyrs nailed to crosses hanging from their rags. Their eyes, full of sorrow, closed in an attempt to parry a blow that was already inevitable.

The corporal gestured to his colleague to examine the woman. Having taken her pulse, the guard shook his head to the accompaniment of the women's murmurs.

'You made a mistake shooting into the air without looking where you were aiming,' said the corporal, touching his nose with a rapacious gesture and spitting on the ground.

'But, Yellow, I...' said the other in an attempt to excuse himself. Yellow, however, interrupted him, talking for everybody.

'He shot into the air, he didn't mean it. You all saw that, didn't you?'

The people fell silent. They were too afraid of that beast to go against him. But Carmucha, who had left the bag of wolfram next to the tree she had hidden behind, came forward, ready to confront him.

'You're a liar. You...'

She didn't have time to say more. Yellow's hand, clenched in a gloved fist, hit her nose violently as a way of shutting her mouth. The impact landed her on the ground like a rag doll for the second time in front of the same man. When she lifted her head to look at the guard, the blood was flowing down the abyss of that beating face, past her lips, towards the thirsty earth, where it mingled with tears.

'Anyone else have anything to say?'

Carmucha looked at him, silently sizing him up. The others kept quiet. Not even the guard falsely accused of firing the shot that had broken Manuela's spine dared to speak. Carmucha lowered her head.

'Come on, out of here, before I start arresting people,' said Yellow.

But nobody moved.

The wake was held in the living room of the big house, but there were so many people they didn't fit, since everybody had come to offer their condolences. I can't tell you how much we loved her. Manuela was a very good girl. Nobody could believe she had died like that, for no reason, crushed by the force of destiny when she was still so young. Matías and Carmucha were very affected, but Félix and Mrs Manuela couldn't even breathe. They didn't have the strength to expand their chests and put that poisoned air in their lungs. Sitting next to the coffin, they received hugs and words of encouragement they didn't even understand. Carmucha, however, understood and didn't want to accept that murder as a tragedy brought about by blind destiny. If destiny was blind, it was because a pig named Yellow had shot at will, unconcerned whether he actually hit anyone. What did he care if he killed somebody? It was said he enjoyed hurting and beating people.

'We have to report him, Papa,' she said to Matías, who sighed, trying to calm her with an embrace, but without agreeing to this impossible undertaking. 'You have to talk to the mayor,' she insisted, not giving up.

Her father took her out of the living room so he could to talk to her away from the others.

'Do you want to get involved in a struggle you won't be able to get out of? Don't you see you're the one who could have died? We're talking about a civil guard in an act of service against some illegal miners.'

Carmucha understood her father was right, but her indignation continued to grow. She spent the night thinking. She spent the day of the funeral as silent as Manuela's grave, but when blackness again took hold of the sky, two shadows slipped into the darkness of an alleyway in the red-light district.

'He's called Coñoño. He's been alone ever since his mother died. We sometimes give him something to carry out errands.' The shadows reached a plot that was strewn with rubbish. Next to a wall was a poorly constructed hovel. It wasn't much more than two doors acting as a roof to keep out the rain. 'He's a good lad, but…' she didn't finish her sentence. They had reached the hovel. 'Coñoño! Coñoño!' called Rebeca.

The effeminate boy Carmucha had seen with Yellow the first time she entered the district emerged from all that misery, gazing at them with a daft expression.

'Carmucha's a friend of mine. She wants to ask you a question.'

The boy scrunched up his nose. He didn't like questions. Carmucha offered him a banknote to overcome his prejudices and the hand advanced with a life of its own until it had grabbed the paper. He folded it and put it away carefully.

'One day I saw you with a man called Yellow. Do you remember him?' The boy shook his head. 'You were in that alleyway. I think he wanted to attack you. Do you remember?'

Then he nodded.

'I don't know his name,' he said in an insecure voice that had been soaked by many storms.

'You don't know who he is?' The boy stared at the ground, hunched over like a frightened dog. Carmucha gave him some more money. 'Have you seen him before?' He took it and nodded. 'Does he give you money when he comes?'

At this point, he looked down and, even though Carmucha took out another note, Coñoño didn't dare carry on talking.

'I don't know anything.'

Carmucha tried to convince him to report Yellow, but understood this was impossible. At least for now.

'Rebeca and I are setting up a school to teach people to read and we want to set up a civic centre. If you can help us…' she again held out the note, 'we could pay you.'

The boy took the note, folded it very carefully, as he had the previous one, and put it in his pocket. He looked at them with a gesture that was equivalent to a smile. They also smiled, thinking they had someone else in their group now, even if it was Coñoño, the idiot who carried out the prostitutes' errands.

The Roman scales balanced out, marking four hundred grams. There was a gentle, siesta-like breeze that rustled the leaves of the trees in a relaxing murmur. Carmucha had ended up accepting there was nothing she could do against Yellow and had gone back to work. She was next to a track that led from the free zone to Cruído and Lousame. It was a wooded place with thick vegetation. She wiped away the sweat with the back of her hand. The gesture reminded her of her dead friend, but she wasn't prepared to succumb to melancholy. She took twenty-six pesetas out of her saddlebag and gave them to the miner, who wasted no time pocketing them and running away. This behaviour struck her as strange. Normally her clients chatted for a while before leaving, promised more merchandise, set about strengthening bonds, but this man had left without even saying goodbye. Carmucha didn't give it any importance and put the wolfram in another saddlebag. She tightened the strap and got ready to mount the horse. Then she saw a man emerging from the oaks that lined the path. He headed towards her, staring at her all the time, a blue cloth hiding his face. She understood she had to get out of there, but the hand of another man, who had arrived from behind without being seen, grabbed the reins. He also had a bluish cloth on his face. A third man came running along the path. His face was a blue stain in motion. Carmucha struggled with the man holding the reins. The man made as if to pull out a knife, but couldn't do so with Carmucha on top of him, kicking, scratching and biting like a ferret. The one running along the path reached them with a revolver in his hand and smashed her in the teeth. The other used this opportunity to grab her hair and yank her to the ground. Carmucha tried to get up, but got a kick in the face that sent her straight to sleep.

When she entered the bar of Roxelio of the priest, her lip was split and swollen, her nose covered in dried blood, her clothes full of earth and her hair tousled. She was a sorry sight, but her appearance caused no impression on the assembled company. This wasn't Noia on a Sunday afternoon. People here always looked a mess. Carmucha stopped in the middle of the bar and searched for Félix among the tables. She immediately found him hidden behind a bottle of liquor. She sat down in silence. They hadn't seen each other since Manuela's funeral and he had spent most of that time sitting there, drinking.

'You sure like getting your face smashed in!' he said with a smile as clear as a river of mud. He took the glass and prepared to take a swig. But she grabbed his hand to stop him.

'I've just been robbed.'

'So? I don't suppose it's the first time, right?' Carmucha nodded with a heavy gesture and kept up the pressure on Félix's arm. 'They must be around here somewhere,' she said, gesturing towards the other tables with her head.

She carried on staring at him because she didn't want to go looking for them, she wanted him to do that. Félix wasn't in the mood, but knew what she was like and realized the only way to get her to leave him alone was to play along. He put the glass on the table and snorted without taking the swig he wanted.

'Their faces were covered with blue cloths,' informed Carmucha.

'The Cobra Gang,' he said, contorting his features. 'Not good news. They pay the guards a commission.' He meant for this reference to the authorities to make her sit back and think. He wanted her to understand that was how things were in this place she didn't belong to. He imagined she had been through enough adventures to tell her grandchildren and could leave now for her father's house to look for a good match. But Carmucha stuck her hand down her cleavage, took out several notes she had hidden there and offered them to him.

'I want you to work for me,' she said stubbornly.

'Why on earth would I work, woman? Can't you see I'm doing very well getting drunk?' said Félix with a sigh of complaint.

'Because you don't like the wolfram ending up in German hands and I don't sell to Montaña. I sell to the English.'

That made a difference. Félix got up and took a swig of liquor.

'Really?' Carmucha nodded, realizing she had hit the nail on the head. 'What do you want?' he asked, immediately forgetting he was drunk.

'To get back what is mine,' she said, but that didn't sound like enough. 'And to carry on buying without getting robbed.'

'The Cobra Gang hang out in a house near Cruído,' he said, sifting the words on his tongue.

The house was a mess. It was built of local stone, poor quality and badly cut, and lots of pieces were missing, which they themselves had taken out. One day, they heard a story and, drunk as they were, started dismantling the house. They thought it was made of rock that had veins of wolfram, like lots of others in the region. They took out the stones before checking to see whether it really contained the black gold everybody was after and, by the time they discovered there was none, the house was half destroyed and they couldn't put it back together again. It was obvious, however, that they still lived there. Hens pecked around, eating and covering the ground with shit. There were tools, cans, bottles and rubbish strewn about, and smoke coming out of the chimney.

Carmucha and Félix reached the front door on foot. They took a deep breath and looked forwards so as not to worry whether they were afraid. Félix emitted a loud shout that was like a grunt and the cigarette in his mouth moved up and down, like a warning flag. A few seconds went by before the door opened and vomited out a man. It was the one who'd hit Carmucha with the pistol.

'What do you want?' he asked bad-temperedly.

'Give me back what you stole from me,' Carmucha tried to appear calm, without sounding threatening, even though she had a stake in her hand. But a stake doesn't pose much of a threat to a man with a pistol. The member of the gang didn't understand this tactic, which set him on edge, giving him an itchy stomach.

'What if I don't want to? Are you going to rob me with a pimp and a stick?'

They didn't move. The other's itching sensation increased, turning into a herd of fears that devoured his insides. They carried on watching him impassively, as if they were very sure of themselves, as if they were expecting reinforcements. When he could no longer control his fear, the thief ran into the house and barred the door. This was the movement they had been waiting for. Félix lit a stick of dynamite with the cigarette in his mouth and started counting with an eye on the fuse.

'One... two... three... four.'

Carmucha watched the fuse burning up. Félix smiled. She was afraid her companion had lost his mind and the dynamite would blow them both to pieces. But he knew what he was doing. He allowed enough time to go by so those inside wouldn't be able to grab the dynamite and throw it back outside. Having got to seven, he came out with the prearranged signal and Carmucha broke the window with the stake. Félix threw the stick of dynamite into the house. At that precise moment, Pepiño of Setes arrived with another two colleagues, all armed with thick, heavy clubs. The five of them took cover, shielded by the stone wall. At this point, the dynamite exploded. What was left of the window flew into the air and landed far away with a crash and the sound of stabbings. The door opened and the members of the Cobra Gang came out one by one, in a daze, the blue cloths around their necks. Some of them were bleeding from their ears owing to the force of the shock wave, and they were all deaf. But when they emerged into the light, as well as deaf, they became blind and were given a warm welcome by Félix's men, who beat them violently until they collapsed on the ground. One of them was left unconscious, the man with the pistol was bleeding like a pig on St Martin's Day, while the third had a broken arm and moaned out loud. Carmucha went up to the man with the pistol.

'I'm going to take what you stole from me – plus expenses,' she said, entering the house.

'And bear in mind the expenses were pretty high!' added Félix, going with her, while the others kept an eye on the wounded.

At the end of summer, everything remained the same. Afternoons in the Casino passed by with deceptive calm. They didn't seem like the afternoons of a world at war. They appeared to float in a placidity that falsely covered the reigning convulsion and anarchy, a convulsion that could only be glimpsed by reading the news from war zones, which seemed to be very far away from Noia. When Carmucha arrived, Colin was scanning the headlines, which, as always, were daunting and sympathetic to the Nazi cause. They talked about a supposedly final attack by the Germans on Stalingrad. Carmucha saw Colin shaking his head and sat beside him, light as a feather and quiet. She watched him, waiting for him to be the one who spoke.

'I see the naughty girl's come back,' he said, enlivened by her presence. 'Where've you been all this time?'

'Working.'

He adopted a condescending tone.

'Oh, right... Don't tell me you're still on about wolfram.' Carmucha nodded. 'How much have you got?'

'Six hundred.'

This figure completely aroused him from his confusion regarding Carmucha, but he pretended not to be impressed.

'Six hundred kilos?'

Carmucha nodded with a satisfied smile.

'The price, however, has gone up. You'll have to pay a hundred and seventy,' she said, staring at him confidently.

Colin's eyes were not very big, but he opened them as wide as he could, taken aback by this girl's character.

'A hundred and sixty,' he offered.

She shook her head. He wasn't really bothered how much he paid, but had to keep up appearances. He offered a hundred and sixty-five and held out his hand, waiting for her to shake it.

Carmucha wanted the money, but after Colin's reaction when she'd offered him her first fifty kilos she was far more interested in gaining his respect. She studied him, trying to work out whether the Englishman's smile contained a glint of irony, but it appeared totally sincere, so she accepted the deal and shook his hand.

'How did you get it?'

Carmucha didn't want to talk to him or be the object of his flirtation. She had the impression she had advanced in her project and that was all that mattered to her. She just wanted to get out of there. She observed him silently, waiting for him to let go of her hand, but when he didn't, she let go of his.

'The material is ready for collection. Let me know when you have the money.' She left a piece of paper on the table with the number of her father's house written in pointy letters and walked out, leaving him feeling utterly perplexed.

Matías was doing his accounts, sitting at the desk in his office, next to the living room in the house in Noia. His nerves betrayed him and he kept getting confused because he feared something would work out badly. He was afraid to sell to the English, afraid his daughter might be attacked, afraid of everything. He heard the sound of wood and looked up, afraid a thief might have come in. But it was Carmucha approaching silently with a leather briefcase. The girl placed the briefcase on the desk.

'I didn't hear the lock,' said her father. She remained silent. 'How did it go?'

Carmucha was a volcano of joy, but endeavoured to appear calm. She was one of those Peléan volcanoes whose lava is so thick it can only come out when the whole mountain explodes. She opened the briefcase, took out 99,000 pesetas in notes and gave them to her father. Matías immediately put them in a metal box, which he then locked.

'Aren't you going to count it?' she asked provocatively.

'I don't think you would want to rob me,' he replied, talking very calmly.

'It wouldn't be a robbery, I earned this with my own work.' Carmucha looked at him, waiting for some congratulations or at least a smile, but when neither one thing nor the other arrived, she turned and left the office. Matías opened his mouth, as if about to say something, but kept quiet and went after her.

'What are you going to do with the money?' he asked when Carmucha was about to emerge from the shadows of the living room. 'With 12,000 pesetas you could go on a wonderful trip.'

'Yes, I could go to Paris on holiday, or even Warsaw. I thought about Stalingrad as well, but I don't think they have any free rooms.'

Matías smiled bitterly at her irony. Both of them knew Paris and Warsaw were occupied by the Nazis; Stalingrad had suffered a long siege with thousands of deaths, and people were afraid it would surrender.

'I was thinking about America.' He fell silent for a while, waiting for his daughter's opinion, but she didn't want to discuss travel. 'You've done it, Carmucha. You've shown me you can do it.' In his tone of voice, there was a 'but'. She waited for it. 'But you're always wandering about, sleeping on your own at the big house… and people talk.' They exchanged suspicious glances. 'Why don't you pack it in? It's not good for a young lady…'

Carmucha felt humiliated. Apart from not receiving any congratulations, she had been obliged to listen to a moral discourse. She didn't let him finish.

'I won't pack it in because we were ruined, Papa. And you don't know how to live without money. I won't pack it in because I like earning a living by my own efforts. And I won't pack it in because when I enter the free zone I sense people's respect.'

'Those who respect you are adventurers and criminals. But what's going to happen to your reputation? What will you do when the war is over?'

Carmucha hadn't thought about the future. She was too young for that. She felt hemmed in by the question and reacted by pulling away from the danger, like a frightened calf.

'Deep down, you've always been afraid of being overshadowed by a woman.'

She left the night of the living room in disappointment, thinking her father didn't value her efforts.

Matías sat in a chair, dead with desperation, afraid his daughter was ruining her future.

Instead of going on holiday, Carmucha bought a house on the outskirts. The house, which had three storeys, had been empty for a while and was in a sorry state, but since she wasn't afraid of work, she cleaned and painted it from top to bottom, with the help of Rebeca, the Ourensan and Coñoño. They sometimes got help from other girls, but few came back – since they weren't normal women, they were used to getting paid for their work and didn't like breaking their backs for no reward.

'Even so, girl, you could have bought a house that wasn't so full of shit,' repeated the Ourensan, who was in the habit of protesting about everything. Carmucha and Rebeca carried on working and laughed when they saw Coñoño, who had more paint stuck to his clothes than he had managed to apply to the walls.

And so the days went by.

After a week, they finished. The women's school now had a home that was modest, but clean and without any obvious damp patches on its walls. Matías also took steps to consolidate the business, but wasn't bothered about the idealist aspects that concerned Carmucha. He fought simply to ensure their survival in a sea full of dangers his daughter knew nothing about. The first thing he did was meet up with the mayor to return the money he'd borrowed. Franco, the Caudillo, who'd assumed all the credit for the military uprising, watched from a portrait that presided over the office in the Casino, as it presided over every office back then.

'There's more money here than I lent you.' Don Severo had just worked out that Matías had added fifteen percent to the amount he owed him, a detail that seemed to please him a great deal.

'Banks would have charged more…' said Matías.

'There was no need,' the mayor interrupted him, trying somewhat unenthusiastically to hand back the commission he'd been given.

'Had they wanted to lend me the money, which they didn't,' Matías vehemently refused to accept the money, putting his hands behind his back, as if the banknotes would burn him.

'All right then, but don't give it any importance. I'm only accepting so as not to offend you.'

The mayor smiled cynically and put away the money. But when he got to his feet, Matías realized he wasn't completely satisfied. He also stood up and the two of them left the office. He waited until they were descending the stairs to the dance hall before continuing their negotiations. The lights were already reaching them, together with the sound of festivities, clinking glasses and jubilant throats.

'I'd like you to be my partner,' he said.

The mayor stopped and looked him in the eyes. He seemed seriously worried.

'You're not selling to the wrong side, are you?' Matías had learned enough patriotic terminology to know how to respond using the official language.

'You know my loyalty is above suspicion. I'm behind the new Europe that takes up arms to put an end to the Marxist threat.'

Severo shook his head ironically, as if that patriotic declaration hadn't been necessary between the two of them, as if such nonsense was only good for public declarations, as a way of deceiving the masses, but not between partners. He talked, in short, as if he knew perfectly well who Carmucha was selling to and as if selling to the other side didn't concern him in the slightest – except for the commercial connotations this decision entailed. He carried on descending the stairs.

'I don't know, Matías. Risking my prestige for the sake of a small commission…' He left the sentence unfinished. The words mingled in the air with the first notes the orchestra was playing. They reached the ground floor.

'That was just a detail, Severo. If we were partners, I would double your commission.'

This was the message Severo had been waiting to hear. He stopped in front of the door where the noise was coming from.

'Matías, you're a patriot!' He moved towards him and gave him a hug. Then, to seal the agreement, he shook his hand eagerly. 'Let us toast the future!' he added, gesturing towards the hall.

After the incident with the Cobra Gang, Carmucha understood she couldn't carry on working in the shadows. Protected by Félix and his team, she started buying in the bar of Roxelio of the priest, where the marketeers bought, paying more or less the same as they did. The extra profit she accrued by lowering her prices to market levels served to ensure the loyalty of Félix and his men, who were paid handsomely. The first few days, Carmucha's arrival put people off. Some said she would bring bad luck; others, that the presence of a woman might attract the attention of the authorities; many, that they couldn't work peacefully if there was a woman about. But people get used to anything; after a while, tongues stopped wagging and eyes stopped looking at her like a strange insect.

Carmucha seemed completely integrated in the business until one afternoon she had a bad feeling. She asked Pepiño if he'd noticed anything. He agreed there was a strange smell in the air and left to have a look around and to talk to Moncho Rañal, who was outside. With the scales ready on the table, Carmucha waited for him to come back, watching the door, but nobody entered. At about five, a miner arrived who had sold her material on previous occasions. The young lad, who can't have been more than twenty, stopped in the doorway and stared at her. His ears stuck out from his head and at that moment they were as red as poppies. He looked at her very seriously, one could almost say fearfully. He then came in, glancing at her from time to time, and went to sit at Miguel Botana's table without saying a single word to her. As he was carrying out the transaction, he continued stealing glances at her as if he wanted to say something, but didn't dare. Carmucha felt the weight of those looks and, without knowing exactly why, began to be worried. She then noticed the other marketeers and the bar owner were also looking at her more than usual. She looked back at the door, but neither Pepiño nor Moncho showed their faces.

Félix's men weren't outside either, in front of the bar as she believed, because having been forced at gun point to accompany four civil guards who had come to fetch them, they were being given a terrible beating. The guards battered them from head to toe, until they had used up all their energy, and left them lying at a bend in the road barely a hundred yards from Roxelio's bar, not bothering to talk or issue warnings. The beating was an explanation in itself, a message as clear as the most inspired poem.

Ten minutes later, Félix entered the bar, worried at not having seen his men at the door, and rushed towards her.

'What the hell is going on? Why are you on your own?' he asked, sitting at the table, speaking in a low voice, trying to appear calm.

'I don't know, but something's wrong.'

She also endeavoured to look calm, in spite of her growing concern.

'I sent Pepiño to have a look. Wasn't he outside the bar?'

'No, he wasn't, and nor was Moncho. Let's get out of here.'

Carmucha gathered her things and left with Félix. As soon as they got outside, seeing no sign of the others, they mounted the horses and abandoned the village at a quick gallop.

In effect, the message was clear, even though it had been written on the faces and backs of members of the team and not on a piece of paper. The meaning was unequivocal, even though Matías had acted dumb in front of Don Severo, with whom he was discussing the circumstances of this action by the Civil Guard.

'I don't understand why they obliged them to move away from the bar,' he said, walking in circles, while Don Severo, seated comfortably at his desk, watched him with an ironic expression.

'That was just a detail, Matías. They were good enough not to beat them in front of people so they wouldn't feel ashamed, you see?' Matías twisted his head as if he didn't understand a thing. 'They want their commission, God damn it! Like every Tom, Dick and Harry. Everybody here gets their share.'

He paused, waiting to hear what Matías thought, who carried on staring silently at the floor, waiting for those words to reach their destination. 'The guards expressed their concern about the regulatory procedure.'

Matías nodded, knowing he had no arguments to contradict what the mayor was saying. He sat down and, opening the drawer, took out the envelope that contained Don Severo's commission. The mayor took it, but, as Matías had foreseen, he did so unwillingly.

'Listen, the way things are going, I have to say I'm not too comfortable with all of this.'

Matías decided to tempt him.

'Because of the amount?'

'Are you off your head, God damn it! If it was a question of money, I'd tell you straight out, it's like you don't know me or something.' He paused, searching carefully for his words. 'It's just, establishing commercial relations like this, without bearing in mind our allies…' he fell silent for a moment to say silently what is never said out loud, 'puts me in a difficult position and…'

Matías understood that second silence as well as he'd understood the first. He'd been waiting for that moment for some time and was ready. He opened the drawer again and took out three more envelopes. He then allowed himself a mischievous smile.

'I had considered that: the military governor, the civil governor and the provincial secretary of the movement,' he said, handing over the envelopes one by one. Don Severo's face lit up as he collected the envelopes and stuffed them in his pocket.

'I always knew you were cut out for politics,' concluded the mayor.

The truth is Matías was holding up as best he could. He sometimes had to go running to the toilets and rush in, kicking open the door of the cubicle, in order then to puke his guts out, his eyes like crystal misted over by vapours of gin, sweating like a sick man, breathing with difficulty, before going back to lick the bottoms of all the Nazis, Fascists and troublemakers that came his way.

The day after his conversation with the mayor, Matías had lunch with his daughter, who couldn't understand what he was doing. She thought her father had changed completely; she thought, with the arrival of the new regime, he had forgotten his ideals and even the memory of his wife. The girl was ashamed of the good humour that dripped off his glassy eyes. She was ashamed of the smiles he directed towards Milagros, a woman in her early forties who had just come to serve in the house, and was ashamed of being his daughter.

Matías gestured politely towards the maid.

'Thank you, Milagros, everything is very good.'

The woman, who hadn't put on a lot of weight, still had an attractive body. She had been in service for sixteen years, ever since her husband died, and had passed through several houses, but this was the first time she had landed in the house of a widower. She had found it difficult to accept the job, being afraid the master might be after something more than cleanliness and order, but when she started working and saw that Matías had no dishonest intentions, she thought she'd never enjoyed so much tranquillity in her professional life and decided never to return to a house where there was a mistress. Milagros picked up the serving tray and left with a slight bow.

'You're going to have to obey the rules,' said Matías to his daughter, who listened while eating her soup and let the words go in one ear and out the other, without leaving the slightest trace on her brain.

'So why don't they arrest them?'

'If they arrest them, they spend a few days in the shadows and the judge gives them a fine of five hundred pesetas for smuggling, but that money goes to the governor, don't you see? It doesn't go to the Civil Guard.' His daughter shrugged her shoulders and Matías continued with his explanations. 'That's not good business. If you're arrested, you don't earn money, which means you can't pay them commission. So they prefer to beat up defaulters to make them see sense.' Carmucha stopped eating. Such an explanation – reasonable, but based on injustice and corruption – disturbed her spirit. 'You'll have to pay. That's the way it's done,' said her father. The girl stood up, turning her head and feet, which walked in circles before and behind the table. 'There are some things you can't fight against, Carmucha.'

That was the problem. She was of an age when the kind of declarations years and experience put in people's mouths were not acceptable. She looked at him and spoke, banging her fist on the table.

'You say that because you're a…' She knew what she wanted to say, but it was her father and she didn't have it in her to say it. 'I won't pay Yellow because he's a lowlife.'

Matías looked at her, softened by her ingenuity.

'If lowlifes couldn't get their share in business transactions, then there would be hardly any commercial activity in the world,' he said with resignation, continuing his meal before his daughter's disbelieving eyes.

Carmucha knew the world was big and it wasn't easy to change it, but she thought she could – at least she knew she felt well when she tried. She felt well when she saw Coñoño playing with a rag doll to entertain the children of two prostitutes who left their offspring in his charge in the secret civic centre. She felt well when she saw them having a good time, used as they were to being left alone in a room while their mothers had to go to work. She felt well explaining to the Ourensan how well the boy managed with them and listening to the other reply, as a joke, that even high-society ladies would end up taking their children somewhere to be looked after. She lived in a feverish state, in a constant struggle against despair, like a soldier ever on the alert, ready to pursue something that gave meaning to her existence crushed by the absence of her mother and the lack of perspective. She couldn't bear the withered world it had fallen to her to live in. But she felt best of all when she was with Rebeca, who told her all the news she heard at work, kept her informed about the changes in the price of wolfram, shared with her rumours about the outcome of the war and served as consolation and inspiration. One day, her friend arrived in a hurry and climbed the stairs to the room where Carmucha was wiping the board before starting class. She sat down next to her and spoke quietly.

'You know what I've just heard?' Carmucha fell silent, correctly imagining that this kind of question precedes important information. 'The employees of the mine are taking out shedloads of wolfram in their pockets, in the folds of their trousers, stuffing it into their clothing. It seems the guards are only concerned to stop people coming in to steal material, and meanwhile the employees are taking it out by the bucketful. In order to avoid being found out, they're selling to marketeers who don't go to the free zone.'

In effect, this information lit up her thoughts and made her change strategy. She decided to visit the mine, which was where the Civil Guard barracks were, and to kill two birds with one stone.

The mine could not be seen in the distance. It was in a hollow, between the twists and turns dug out in the mountain by the river, forming a mixed bunch of diverse buildings. There were workshops for carpenters and blacksmiths, rooms full of machines that washed and separated the mineral from the earth, offices of various kinds, an infirmary and living quarters. Even the entrance to the underground tunnels had its own building which gave access to the main gallery. This in turn led to different caves that penetrated the earth like bronchi. The galleries formed a lung whose breath ran along the ventilation shafts, climbing outside from the depths, ferrying oxygen and allowing the moles that worked night after night to breathe, since the sun never reached that place. And finally there were the Civil Guard barracks, which were located in the mine to defend the interests of the Germans and their friends and allies, both declared and clandestine.

Carmucha and Félix approached the entrance, which was watched over by a guard, on foot. It was so hot that day the very stones seemed to be sweating.

'You have to be nice, remember. And don't even think about discussing politics!' Carmucha insisted on her instructions because she didn't trust her bodyguard's impulsive nature.

'Come off it, woman, half of them were comrades in the CNT trade union,' he said to calm her down while wiping the sweat with his hand.

'It doesn't matter. Ask them how much they sell for and offer a little more.' Carmucha spoke with great authority, without the need to raise her voice, as if she was much older than she was. The guard, his uniform darkened by patches of sweat, came out to meet them with an expression that was serious, threatening almost, and certainly not very friendly.

'Afternoon.'

'Good afternoon. We came to greet some friends and to talk to the guards,' said Carmucha, accompanying her words with a gesture and offering her hand to be shaken. On the palm, clear for all to see, was a folded note. The guard observed her hand. He then looked at the faces of these visitors, who smiled, wagging their tails like two sweaty dogs. He let a few seconds go by, which seemed eternal, and finally decided to take the note while shaking the girl's hand. He gave them free passage.

Félix, who knew the area very well, went to greet a couple of men rolling cigarettes in the shade. Carmucha carried on wandering around the mine and soon reached a kind of square with the offices, the infirmary and the house of Don Teo, the doctor. She had met him the day Manuela died, but had heard about him before that, since he was very much loved by all the wolfram people. Don Teo was hired by the mine to look after the workers' health, but he didn't just look after the miners, he also attended to anyone in need, even if they were illegal workers, and refused to charge poor families. From there, she could see the building where the barracks were. There was a guard on duty at the door.

'May I see the corporal?' she asked when she reached him.

She was shown to a small, empty, sad room that was typical of military barracks. She looked at the flaking white walls and waited, allowing the sweat to run down her face without drying it, trying to forget the suffocating heat. A little while later, a door opened and in came the shit-coloured guard. He approached her, fixing her with his eagle eyes, cold and silent as a knife. Carmucha handed him an envelope. Yellow looked inside. It was full of notes, but he didn't bother counting them. There would be time for that.

'Is it enough?' asked Carmucha, disturbed by his silence.

The guard, who didn't seem satisfied with the amount, stuffed the envelope in his pocket.

'Come back next month,' he said and waited for her to leave.

But Carmucha wasn't ready yet. She wanted to gouge out those serpent eyes right there, in the barracks, and carried on staring at him without moving, challenging him. It drove her mad that the guard should act as if it was the first time he'd seen her, despite the fact he'd bashed her face in a couple of times and they were both perfectly aware he knew her. In the end, when Yellow gestured contemptuously to her to leave, Carmucha, without taking her eyes off those puddles of poison, carefully wiped the sweat off her forehead with the back of her hand and went outside.

Things carried on like this, and autumn came. Carmucha was respected by the guards and continued buying in Roxelio's bar, as well as buying directly from the workers of the mine, who took wolfram out in their pockets, in the lining of their jackets, in the turn-ups on their trousers and even in bags hidden beneath their caps and hats. I have to admit the Englishman was trustworthy, kept his word and bought everything she managed to gather.

And so winter arrived. Carmucha continued buying and selling without rest and continued working in the civic centre. She continued visiting her mother's grave and kept her informed of her progress and novelties. She told her how, following the idea of the red-light-district nursery, they also gathered the mining women's children so they wouldn't be alone when their mothers went 'robbing', which was how they referred to this illegal activity. The little ones were looked after by Mrs Manuela, who after her daughter's death was grateful for any activity that kept her busy and stopped her thinking. Carmucha told her mother, however hard she tried, she couldn't get Mrs Manuela to accept any money for doing that job, which she said gave her life. She also told her how at the women's school, apart from teaching them to read and write, they taught sewing, cooking and anything else they could, since if any girl had a particular skill, she would teach the others, and that was how things were organized.

Carmucha felt well doing that job. She felt well fighting to help improve people's misery, but when she came back to the sad house she shared with her father, she was still far too anguished inside to talk to him openly. Unconsciously, the two of them maintained the status quo they had reached after the differences that arose when the wolfram fever began. They loved each other a great deal and knew this confrontational situation could only be temporary. They shared a house and shared the wolfram business, but were incapable of sharing their deepest thoughts. They limited themselves to discussing the situation, commercial strategies, the dangers that beset them, but never seriously undertook the task of overcoming their differences by telling one another how much they loved and needed each other. No doubt because they both believed this confrontation was as nothing compared to the affection they professed for each other. They were both stubborn and let the time go by. And so spring came around, and then the summer of 1943.

Although there were few changes in Noia, things were changing on the world stage. During that winter, the sixth army of the Wehrmacht, which until then had seemed pretty invincible, was annihilated in Stalingrad together with a regiment of their Croatian allies, two Romanian divisions and an anti-aircraft division of the German air force. Under the orders of General Paulus, they fought to the death, without skimping on a single cartridge, until complete annihilation, or so they said. It was alleged General Winter had tipped the battle in favour of the Russians, as it had done to defeat Napoleon, but whatever the reason, the defeat was highly painful. The efforts of the Nazi Minister of Propaganda to twist the meaning of that defeat didn't help much. In the paper, his photograph appeared next to the name of Doctor Goebbels. I suppose they called him 'doctor' so the title would give him the appearance of a good man, in an attempt to circumvent the obvious vampiric look his image revealed. I wish you could have seen that photo. Really, all he needed was a pair of fangs to resemble a perfect vampire. The fact is, with the same cynical, deceitful style as always, he gave speeches, declaring how a blow like this would serve only to strengthen Germany even more, having recovered from such a great misfortune, it would be completely invincible. He said this because he knew people were beginning to think the exact opposite. They were beginning to think perhaps the Germans weren't as invincible as they seemed. That devil was a genius of political propaganda. It may sound strange, but that style is still in use today. It's a question of denying the evidence as barefacedly as possible and accusing those who tell the truth of being liars. It's a style used by dictatorships, but it also serves to keep the rank and file of your party in order after an electoral defeat or other important setback. After that, they alter their discourse, counting on the fact collective memory is weak, and try to grow once more.

The weather improved and the situation began to deteriorate in Italy. There was no way of blaming General Winter for that. In July, the news arrived of Mussolini's resignation. Pessimism began to proliferate among some of the greatest defenders of international fascism, but in the Casino life carried on merrily as usual and the money continued to flow. Matías had swapped his old, worn suit for others that were handmade, but he carried on playing poker with his everyday companions.

'I'm out of luck, there's just no way,' said Don Rüdiger, tossing his cards on the table. The pessimism in his dark eyes was plain to see.

'Unlucky at cards…' Matías tried to encourage him, but the German didn't react.

'It's not that. I'm out of luck. I just don't like the way things are going.'

Before this veiled complaint, Matías looked at his cards and, even though he had three sevens, put them face down on the table, as the German had done, pretending to share the same misfortune.

'I'm out of luck as well,' he said, looking at Don Severo, who was also waiting for an explanation for the remark the Montaña representative had made.

'The marketeers are selling to the English,' indicated the Teuton with a vague gesture towards the table where the British met.

Don Severo opened his eyes and mouth as if he had just heard a blasphemy.

'How shameful! What a lack of patriotism…! After going through a war and suffering the same dishonour on account of the same people as always.' The mayor seemed really indignant, but Don Rüdiger paid him no attention and just picked up the little money he had left on the cloth. 'Anyway, I suppose the amounts are small, the main dealers are people of proven morality.'

'Money is stronger than morals,' cut in the German, causing the mayor to shut up. Rüdiger shrugged his shoulders. He looked beaten.

'Don't say that, Don Rüdiger,' said Matías, trying to come to his partner's aid with a distracting manoeuvre.

'It doesn't matter, we will match the English price. Good night.' Don Rüdiger departed, leaving Matías and Don Severo pondering their own complicity.

'I think we should buy a mine,' said Matías.

'We don't have that much.' In his dreamy tone, it was clear the mayor would be happy if he could do that.

'I mean an exhausted mine.' This clarification brought a frown to Don Severo's face. 'We could declare some false production and sell it to the Germans.'

'But false production doesn't exist, why would they want to buy it?'

'Because the wolfram they extract legally from our mines is not enough… That's why they buy from marketeers as well. With our false quota, they could turn part of the smuggled material into legal mineral. That would help with the customs procedures and greatly decrease the cost of transport.' Matías twisted his mouth, making an ironic gesture.

Don Severo understood his idea.

'And it would leave us in a very comfortable position,' he said, considering the consequences of such a purchase.

Matías nodded.

'Exactly. We would play with two packs. We would sell wolfram to one side and a lie to the other, but both would be profitable for them and for us,' he added by way of conclusion.

The mayor's expression revealed his interest, even though he knew it wouldn't be easy to put such an idea into practice.

'The bad thing is people try to take advantage. I've heard they're asking crazy prices for mines that produce almost nothing. Real immoralities, I'm telling you!' The mayor sighed, thinking about such profiteers. 'We would have to force them to lower their price.'

After this sentence, pronounced with an ambiguous gesture, he stared at Matías, as if seeking his advice or giving him free rein to act as he saw fit. Matías, who had drunk several glasses of gin, nodded as if he understood perfectly without the need to discuss details – details his partner wasn't interested in and didn't want to know.

The consequences of those words soon turned into facts. Ever since she'd got involved in trafficking, Carmucha would visit Rita's place from time to time, without disguising or hiding herself, almost always accompanied by Félix as a bodyguard. She liked to affirm her autonomy by paying these bizarre visits which she used to close some business deal or to chat to the prostitutes. That night, she arrived with an uneasy mind. She was eager to close the deal that had brought her there. She sat at the counter, next to Rebeca, and ordered a drink. She was very excited, almost happy, but could see a net full of anxiety in his friend's eyes.

'Everything will be all right, don't you worry,' she said to the blonde, who shook her head while swallowing saliva.

'It's not that, Carmucha. The thing is I have some news to tell you.'

At this point, a man came up, ready to start a conversation, but Carmucha eyed him with such fury he was intimidated.

'Forgive me for interrupting.'

'Get out of here. Can't you see the young lady's with me?'

The client ran away in shame and went to join a circle where he shared remarks with other men who were as drunk as he was. They laughed scandalously and came out with whispers, like children discussing sex behind their parents' backs, because hearing Carmucha say the young lady was with her was like hearing the devil speak. Those words could mean only two things: she was a client and therefore had the same right as the man to engage with the girl without being disturbed, or she was another worker and had a right to chat quietly for a moment without being disturbed by the clients. Either possibility seemed unacceptable. That said, they believed the former was more likely, so they laughed, calling her a butch, someone who pees standing up, and stuff like that. They hadn't considered a third possibility, which was the real one, where Carmucha wasn't a client or a worker, but just a friend, because no woman back then would have done such a thing if she wanted to be accepted in society. Carmucha, however, didn't care what they thought and gazed at Rebeca, questioning her with her look, waiting for her to go on.

'I met this guy. He wants me to stop being a prostitute and to go with him to Barcelona.' Rebeca saw Carmucha's eyes growing moist and added in an apologetic tone, 'He's very good to me.'

Carmucha felt herself go weak. During those months, Rebeca had been the person she'd shared her deepest feelings with, her mainstay in order to confront difficulties. Hearing that news filled her with joy because she wanted her to be happy. The chance to leave that work sounded like a unique opportunity, but on the other hand the idea of her going far away destroyed her inside. They gave each other an emotional hug, which was followed by a chorus of titters from the drunks, who were watching them eagerly.

'I'll miss you so much!'

Rebeca also cried in her arms. A woman who was quite a bit older than the rest came up to talk to them in private. She moved with the elegance and grace of first youth, though reality belied her wish to keep her figure intact.

'Dinner is served.'

The girls released each other. Carmucha dried the tears on the back of her hand and, very discreetly taking out a wad of notes from her cleavage, handed it surreptitiously to the other woman, who took them.

'This is your home,' she said.

'Thanks, Rita.'

Carmucha escaped all the emotion by gesturing towards Félix, who was waiting in a corner of the bar, and the two of them headed towards the corridor that led to the rooms, like other couples going in and out of that corridor. But they weren't after a bed, they were after the dinner Rita had talked about. This was a dinner that had just been cooked in one of the rooms, where a squat, overweight man in his fifties was letting himself be undressed by a young, pretty prostitute who could barely read or write. The girl wanted to stop being ignorant and formed part of Carmucha's clan. She was about to give the man's flaccid stomach a few licks while letting her hands slip into his pants in order to take them off when the door opened abruptly.

To the man's surprise, Félix and Carmucha appeared with cloths on their faces. Moments later, in came Pepiño of Setes, covered in the same way, closing the door behind him. The three of them launched themselves at the dinner like three hungry lions. They pushed the prostitute aside, with just the right amount of violence so as not to hurt her, but with sufficient force so she wouldn't look like an accessory, and immobilized the man on the bed. His inability to move, his nakedness and the fear he felt prevented him from defending himself. He watched as Félix and Pepiño tied his feet and hands to the bed legs, getting more and more frightened, but still not daring to utter a word. Carmucha came up to his ear.

'What would your wife say if she could see you now?'

Pepiño took out the large knife he always carried and started cleaning his nails. He did this as if he was sitting in a meadow, watching the cows graze, without the slightest threatening gesture. But he wasn't in a meadow and the fat man thought he was going to die, even if it was just out of fear. He swallowed and tried to reply to Carmucha, who carried on looking at him, a couple of inches from his face, but the words got stuck in his throat as he glanced nervously at those unknown eyes that held him prisoner.

'And your daughter? What would your daughter have to say?'

Carmucha moved back a little, allowing him to see the door through which Moncho de Rañal came in, carrying a leather wineskin. Moncho, as covered and quiet as Félix's other men, approached the fat man and emptied the wineskin, which was full of pig blood, on his head. The blood dripped down his face, entered his mouth and made him cough, while he endeavoured to spit out that thick, almost clotted concoction. The others watched in silence. The spectacle was unpleasant for everybody.

'What do you want?' the fat man finally managed to blurt out.

'We want justice,' replied Carmucha.

The man still didn't understand a thing. He was getting more and more frightened. The blood covered his chest and spread like a red sheet.

'Why the hell do you want the mine if it's exhausted? Can't you see deep down they want to do you a favour, my turtledove?' said Félix, coming up to the man's face, but a look from Carmucha made him return to his place.

'You received an offer for the mine, right?' said the girl. The fat man nodded vigorously, on the verge of tears. 'Was it not a reasonable offer?' The man glimpsed an exit and threw himself towards it, praying silently to God that this would not be the disagreeable epilogue to a comfortable life.

'Yes, yes. It was a good offer.'

'But you wanted to take advantage of the fact everything's a mess to charge much more than the mine is worth, and that's an injustice, right?'

'I'm very sorry. I'll sign the contract tomorrow. I promise!'

The anguish in his eyes was plain to see. Anguish and terrible fear. Carmucha didn't enjoy this vision. She would have liked to apologize, but realized that would have been a mockery. She glared at the prostitute, who was still hunched up next to the wall they had thrown her against.

'Untie him,' she said before gesturing to the others to leave at once.

When Rebeca left for Barcelona, Carmucha felt more alone than ever. She hadn't yet turned nineteen, but she had these moments when she was overwhelmed by melancholy, nostalgically recalling the old times as if she was an old woman. She often went riding, crossing the fields and paths at full gallop, always at dawn or sunset, her dark silhouette outlined against the violet sky, as if with these races she might leave behind the nostalgia squeezing her chest. But the anguish ran as fast as her horse and she couldn't get rid of it. Mountain people got used to these outbursts of speed, got used to watching her pass like a dark arrow in those moments of ambiguous light, and started coming up with reasons for these journeys. Her attitude the day Manuela was killed had given her a reputation as a brave and just woman, because she was the only one who had stood up to Yellow. She hadn't lowered her head like the others. Apart from that, she paid the highest prices for the wolfram and never tried to take advantage of the workers. People, who needed hope, wanted to believe there was a kind of defence in these races for the miners against the all-powerful and corrupt forces of the law and government. So her fame took off, passing from mouth to mouth, the way legends begin. Some said she travelled to warn if the guards were about to carry out a raid; others went further and said if she had been out at dawn, there would be no danger that day. If anyone saw her black silhouette running at sunset, they would sleep peacefully, thinking the next day luck would be on their side and they would find a good vein. 'There goes Carmucha from the big house,' they would remark, 'we'll be lucky today.'

Other times, instead of racing on her horse like a woman possessed, she would go out with Félix for a gentle ride. She was almost always quiet, gazing at the lands with curiosity and attention, as if she'd never seen them before. On one of those days, she took him to a place away from the tracks, where there was a crag from which you could contemplate a good portion of the small valley, which was at the edge of the free zone. Among the rocks, there was a narrow, elongated cave which you could get to through a crack. The entrance was shielded by laurels and a group of oaks that had buried their roots in among the stones. Once inside, you could see out through gaps in the rocks, which made the cave a lookout or, if you prefer, a secret castle.

Carmucha dismounted.

'It's here. My father showed it to me when I was a girl,' she said to Félix, who knew the cave, but pretended he was seeing it for the first time.

They both went in through the narrow passageway that gave access to the cave. Carmucha stared at that space as if it was a cathedral, with the eyes of a little girl.

'I used to have such a good time...' She went up to a gap in the rocks and put her hand in a hole. 'Look, I kept it here just in case.' From the darkness, she extracted a small chestnut box tied with string that was half rotten.

Félix watched her in amusement.

'It seems to me you're going to have to swap it for a suitcase of money and a pistol.' Félix wanted to crack a joke, but the joke was left unanswered. At that moment, they heard a shot. The two of them rushed towards the hole that faced in the direction the shot had come from.

Further down, among the vegetation, they saw a woman running away from a civil guard who was chasing her with his shirt unbuttoned. Carmucha was about to go running out to help her, but Félix's hand grabbed her arm, holding her in the cave. They then heard the woman's laughter.

'Don't get involved,' said Félix with an angry gesture. 'It's either that or go hungry.' Carmucha stared at him, open-mouthed. 'The women and their families.'

Coming out from behind a tree, another guard arrived, also accompanied by a mining woman, and the two of them disappeared from view as they fell into the vegetation.

'They pay them like this to let them work?' asked Carmucha with a gesture that combined surprise with indignation and disgust.

'That's right! They wouldn't screw them for pleasure, now, would they, given the way they treat us?'

Félix was annoyed. He was ashamed at this situation as if it was a part of his own family that was obliged to prostitute itself.

Carmucha fell silent for a moment, drumming her cheek with her fingers, before asking Félix:

'Yellow doesn't do that, does he?'

Félix didn't understand the reasons that led her to ask this question, but was surprised at her perspicacity.

'How did you know?' Carmucha didn't reply, but he could see in her eyes she wanted to know more. 'They say he watches, but doesn't actually...' Félix's cheeks were burning. 'Look, I don't know how to say it to you, but you understand what I mean, don't you?'

'And the shot?'

'That was so nobody would come and make them... lose the thread, you know?'

Félix sat down with a sigh, attempting to bring this awkward conversation with a young lady to an end. Carmucha clenched her teeth tightly, sounding like an unoiled door closing slowly.

'We'd better wait a while before leaving,' said Félix, gazing at the ground of damp stone.

Three unkempt children raced across the living room of the big house, screaming like wild beasts. Mrs Manuela ran after them to take them to the kitchen and wash their faces. Matías watched with a half smile on his lips, listening to the curses of the woman, who was crazy about them, despite her apparent bad temper. Matías' face darkened, however, when through the window came the sound of horse hooves, signalling Carmucha and Félix's arrival. He went up to the window and saw his daughter and the bodyguard gazing curiously at a black vehicle parked in front of the house. The girl dismounted and led the horse towards the stable.

When Matías came in, Carmucha had just taken the saddle and saddlebags off the horse, which was panting, thinking about the straw that was waiting in its stall. The girl gave the horse a slap and looked at her father.

'I see you have a driver now.'

'It's important in business to keep up appearances.'

Carmucha went to give him a kiss and found him rigid, far too distant. Even though their differences were still entrenched, hidden beneath the surface of silent normality that linked them, the absence of complications and the recent money had improved their relations. Carmucha continued working.

'I haven't seen you for days,' said Matías with a gesture of reproach. Carmucha shrugged her shoulders and carried on taking the mineral out of the saddlebags and placing it in a stall that didn't have animals, but wolfram.

'I'm going to up the Englishman's price. I'm sure he can pay two hundred and fifty.'

Matías wasn't prepared to let her change the subject, moving away from the topic that concerned him.

'The other day you were seen at Rita's... in the company of a woman.' Matías spoke, looking at the ground, ashamed to hear what he himself was saying.

'It runs in the family, Papa,' she replied with the irony she had developed ever since hooking up with Félix again. It was the wild irony of people from the free zone.

Matías took a step forward, putting himself between the horse and his daughter so she would stop working and talk to him. Carmucha went around him and carried on working.

'You promised not to cause any more scandals.'

'I didn't go to Rita's to cause a scandal, I went to do a job,' she said, taking a saddlebag. Matías gave it a kick, knocking it to the ground and spilling the mineral that was inside. In this way, he got Carmucha to look at him.

'You didn't need to do it yourself, Carmucha.'

'You got your mine, didn't you?'

'But there's no need to run useless risks,' he said, failing to recognize the merit she deserved in having achieved the objective he had marked out. Once again, she waited for a word of gratitude or congratulations, but instead of this her father stared at her severely. 'And I suppose you had to cuddle up and kiss a prostitute in front of everybody else?'

'It was Rebeca, Papa. She told me she was leaving for Barcelona and I gave her a hug. There was no kiss. You should know facts get deformed when stories are passed from mouth to mouth.'

Matías was glad to hear this, mainly because he didn't like his daughter being friends with such people, as he said so as not to say 'whores'. Carmucha realized what he was thinking and felt offended. She didn't understand why he had so little respect for her wishes and inclinations when it came to choosing company.

'You're on a bad path, Carmucha, I'm just trying to warn you,' he said, lowering his tone of complaint just a little.

'You also could have warned Mother you were going to betray her, but you didn't. The trouble with you, Papa, is you never loved anybody – either her or me!'

Carmucha left the stable in a fury, feeling misunderstood and despised by her father. Matías stayed in the shed, kicking and punching tools in desperation and uttering curses.

That night, he didn't go down to Noia. He stayed in the big house, drinking gin straight out of the bottle and staring at a photograph of his wife while listening to the voices of the dogs, which barked in the distance and were muffled by the murmuring wind. He tried to find a way for his daughter to understand things, to understand him. But what he knew about life was so different from what Carmucha knew that communication seemed impossible. He tried to protect her, he wanted her to carry on being a girl, to carry on believing her mother was perfect, but it broke his heart that she should think he was a devil.

A few days later, Carmucha had gathered enough material to go back to the Casino. She went as soon as she finished her class in the red-light district and arrived before the dance had started. It didn't even occur to her to get changed. It was still hot and she was sweaty. She was longing to go home and slip into a bath. She would have liked to get in with her clothes on, wearing the same blue suit she'd been wearing since the night before, and drink a jug of ice-cold beer.

Next to the dance floor was her big-nosed friend with another two girls. The three of them were wearing print dresses with pleated skirts, tight waists and anxious necklines. Their suits were cut and sewn with the unequivocal aim of catching the young men's attention and arousing their desire, but they pretended to behave like novice nuns. Carmucha hadn't seen Maribel since the incident I told you about, so she used the fact her mother was absent to go and talk to her. When she said good evening, both Maribel and the other two doves looked the other way, pretending not to have seen or heard her, as if she was a ghost. Carmucha couldn't understand why she was receiving this treatment she didn't think she deserved. It was one of the negative results of being different from others and not just following the crowds and their fashions. She was about to demand an explanation, but realized the big-nosed girl was sweating profusely and was much more embarrassed than she was, and felt sorry for her. She decided to leave her with her two clucking hens, warming the nest in the hopes of finding a young cockerel prepared to mount their henhouse. She went to sit at the bar, near the Englishmen's table. Colin was reading the paper. When he saw her, he ordered something and sat on a stool beside her.

'Do you have something for me?' The Englishman had drunk too much that afternoon and was inclined to play the game of double meanings.

'Of course. Otherwise I wouldn't be here with you.'

'Do you never come to have fun?'

Carmucha glanced at a paper lying on the counter. On the cover was a small black-and-white photograph of a German submarine, barely a black silhouette outlined against a confused sky. On deck could be glimpsed a solitary man like a lost sentinel, about to drown when the boat disappeared underwater.

'It's not the time to be having fun.'

'It's precisely times like this when people most want to have fun,' he retorted, grabbing the glass of whisky the waiter had just served him and downing it at once.

'I have another consignment, but you'll have to pay two hundred and fifty,' replied Carmucha, not wanting to get involved in his game.

'What does the money matter? That's what war's about, right?' Carmucha noticed Colin was having difficulty talking due to the amount of alcohol in his body. 'It's a question of frittering away money while people die from a shot, drowning or hunger. The way they die doesn't matter so much, it's the fact they die that's important.' His scepticism produced in him these bitter reflections and the alcohol gave him wings to bring his body close to hers in an insinuating manner.

Carmucha was surprised by the ease with which he accepted the increase in prices. She thought the reason for his lack of resistance had to do with the fact she was a woman. Perhaps that was why Colin tried to get closer than he should, because he thought his willingness in business terms might earn him some sexual compensation. Carmucha wasn't in the mood to find out if this supposition was true or not. She left him with the words in his mouth. For her, everything to do with sex had a negative connotation at that time, because all the sex she ever saw was bought or forced, violent in some way or depraved by relations of power and money. It wasn't a question of whether she liked the Englishman or not, she just didn't like the idea of getting physical and intimate with anybody. What really obsessed her was the fever to get more wolfram. Nor was it a question of making money for the women's school, which functioned without problems, or to fight for her right to act independently, as her mother had taught her. By this stage, the wolfram fever had taken hold of her like an illness. Many people suffered from this illness and the fevers it provoked. They went crazy and rushed ahead without looking where they were going. They acted like madmen entering the motorway the wrong way or like the kamikazes that had yet to leave their mark on the Pacific War. They persisted down their path until coming across an inevitable obstacle. On Carmucha's path, that obstacle was Yellow, who got in the way and trampled on her rights. Yellow drove her beside herself.

The day after the conversation with Colin, Carmucha arrived at the bar of Roxelio of the priest with Félix. She sat in her usual place, took the scales out of her shoulder bag and placed her things on the table. At the counter, she saw two girls she knew from the free zone. Their hair had been totally shaved.

'Have you seen them?' asked Carmucha.

'That's what they do to women who can't pay and won't open their legs.' Félix said this as a joke, the way he always did when talking about the sad things of life, the things you must throw on your back if you wish to keep going without becoming bitter. Carmucha, however, hadn't learned to do that yet. Her eyes filled with hatred.

At that precise moment, Yellow came in. He sometimes went there for a drink. Roxelio's bar enjoyed a kind of unofficial neutral status. I suppose that must have cost Roxelio a certain amount of money. Yellow never arrested anybody there, but his attitude towards the assembled company was that of a tyrant. He resembled a pharaoh because, when he came in, people lowered their heads and stared at the ground to avoid meeting his eyes, which is what you told me used to happen in the Egyptian court.

Yellow sauntered between the tables, glad to see his subjects were staring at the floor in a cowardly fashion. He reached the counter and the waiter served him a drink without him having to say a word or make a gesture. The shaven-headed women gave up their place and moved to the back. The bar sank into silence. Félix looked at Carmucha, afraid that she would do something stupid.

'Please, Carmucha, don't look at him,' he whispered when he saw the girl couldn't keep her eyes down.

Yellow finished his drink in one go and, still glancing over his shoulder at the people at the tables, waved to Roxelio and headed for the door. As he walked, he saw the backs of the necks of his followers until he got to where Carmucha was seated, who, much to Félix's displeasure, couldn't help looking up at him. The civil guard came to a halt.

'I don't suppose you have wolfram in that bag, do you?' Everybody had wolfram in their bags and pockets, but he asked this as if the fact of carrying wolfram in a bag was something abnormal and reckless.

'So what if I do?' The arrogance on Carmucha's face was masked when Yellow wrote a response on it with his open hand. Félix took a deep breath to resist the natural impulse to hit the guard back, who didn't even look at him as he searched the bag. When he saw it was empty, he tossed it to the ground. Carmucha was bleeding profusely through her nose again.

'You need a permit to transport wolfram, and everybody here knows I'm the one who issues permits.' He fell silent to watch the girl wipe the blood away with her hands and waited until she looked at him again. When their eyes met, he issued this warning: 'You should be more careful.'

He then continued to the door. As soon as he left, people started uttering curses and spitting on the floor. Félix looked at Carmucha, unable to contain the irony in his eyes. An irony that suggested he had warned her already. He kept quiet, however, and offered her his handkerchief that smelled of gunpowder.

'Just don't say anything, OK?' she remarked.

Félix tried to remain serious, but a reflex movement on his chin gave away the effort he was making not to burst into laughter.

After that unpleasant incident, luck changed. It seemed as if the mountain people had agreed to make it up to her and almost all those who arrived went to sell at Carmucha's table. By two in the afternoon, her shoulder bag was full of wolfram. She thought about going for a ride to make the most of the good weather before the summer ended and Félix offered to go with her.

The earth was very dry, crying out for the arrival of the autumn rains, but the heat wasn't in a hurry to leave. The horses kicked up lots of dust, even though they were only trotting along. They slowly entered a forest, getting away from the sun. They followed a path that winded beneath the crowns of the trees and, as they rounded a bend, next to an open field with a ramshackle hut, they came across two civil guards who grabbed their horses' reins. Another guard gestured with his rifle for them to get down. In front of the hut was Yellow, accompanied by another two guards and two mining women, who looked down when they saw them arrive. The guard with the rifle pushed them in the back towards the hut.

'We're going to teach the young lady some manners.' Having said this, Yellow signalled to a guard to take her into the hut.

Félix tried to defend her, but before he could take a step he was hit so hard by the butt of the rifle that he collapsed on the ground, as quiet and still as a sleeping baby. The civil guard grabbed Carmucha by the arm and led her towards the hut. She didn't resist until she was next to Yellow. Then she dug her feet in the ground to talk to him.

'Come with me if you're a man,' she said, spitting hatred in his shit-coloured face. Yellow held her gaze for a while before accepting the challenge. He walked towards the door of the hut and opened it, inviting her in with an ironic gesture of politeness. Carmucha shrugged off the guard who was holding her and entered, followed by Yellow.

Inside, there was just a dilapidated table and a bed with a kind of straw mattress. Carmucha leaned against the table with a look of defiance.

'What are you waiting for to get undressed?' said the civil guard.

'I want to propose a deal.'

Yellow let out his twisted smile to give his answer a double meaning.

'What the fuck would you have that might interest me, you wretch?'

'I know things,' she said, staying calm.

'Talk.' He paused to let out another laugh. 'Or pull down your knickers.'

'I know you like young boys. I saw you with one next to Rita's. I also know it was you who killed Manuela. If you want me to keep your secret, you'll have to let me not pay you anymore.' Yellow remained mute, but it wasn't out of fear, as Carmucha thought, it was out of surprise at the girl's naivety. 'What are you going to do when everybody finds out you're queer?'

Yellow threw himself at her without answering and grabbed her by the neck as if he intended to strangle her. Carmucha opened her mouth to breathe and he used this opportunity to stick his tongue in her mouth the way a serpent slides into a hole. He then spat on the ground and gave her a slap that made her coil like a burning leaf. He then grabbed her by the hair and pulled her down, so her forehead collided with the table, before brutally lifting her skirts.

'Who the hell are you to know what I like?' he said, yanking down her knickers, digging the seams into her flesh. Carmucha tried to turn around, but the civil guard had her under control. At that moment, she understood she was going to go through Calvary and completely lost her strength. She heard the civil guard bringing up saliva and carefully spitting on one hand before using it as a lubricant.

'You're going to go about, telling people I killed an illegal miner? What do you think you'll achieve? What you're doing is illegal. I can kill you all if I want to.' The guard spoke in bursts, pausing because of the effort he was making to rape her. Carmucha didn't resist, but carried on sweating because of the effort she had made to defend herself. She focused her thoughts on the drops running down her forehead and watched them falling on the table, in front of her devastated eyes, trying to endure the pain and humiliation with dignity. She wanted to keep that at least in front of her enemy. 'You can tell them this as well when you go around saying I'm queer, don't you think?' he said between thrusts.

Carmucha didn't reply, but swore then and there she would have her revenge. As she swore, the tears sprang into her eyes.

That afternoon, when she got home, Matías was in his armchair, reading a novel. In the darkness of the living room, he couldn't see his daughter's eyes were red from crying. Carmucha went over to give him a kiss, a kiss like every day, though she needed much more than that. She put her hand next to his and looked at the title of the novel. It was *The Crime of Father Amaro* by Eça de Queiroz. Carmucha sought out his eyes, but, still annoyed by her attitude regarding the mine, he just carried on reading. She sighed before deciding to seek comfort by taking her father's hand. Just as she made up her mind and started moving her hand to take his, her father got up. Their hands crossed in the air like two directionless messenger pigeons. Carmucha pulled hers back as if it had been bitten. Before going out, Matías stopped in the doorway and said he had a meeting at the Casino.

They were going through the most difficult time in their relationship. When children stop being young in order to fully become adults, they no longer know their parents. The paternal figure they had in their childhood no longer serves to calibrate them. And yet they still don't know the adult world well enough to understand that person who suddenly seems like a stranger. Parents go through more or less the same thing. They can't accept that their child has changed and is no longer an unbreakable follower of their paternal opinions. Nor can they work out their child's true nature until the passing of a few years has given them their adult character, and they die of fear, thinking they might lose them forever. Both sides feel they are under attack. Beforehand, everything was clear, and suddenly chaos has taken hold of their relationship. A relationship that has been so intimate and important in their lives threatens to change completely and both sides think it's for the worse. They almost always believe it's the other's fault, and besides they're convinced they have plenty of time to solve the problem. Sometimes they pass up opportunities that won't come back.

The two of them waited for a gesture from the other to break the tension. Carmucha wanted to run towards him and throw herself in his arms, but she didn't do this. Her father was longing for a hug from his daughter, but thought he deserved an apology before showing her affection. Matías left without another word.

Carmucha slept badly. She sweated and twisted and turned in the bed like a downtrodden worm. She woke up in the early hours. The rancid light of a street lamp lit her room from below, slipping through the gaps in the shutter, giving the room a ghostly appearance. She had been jumping and running in her nightmare for some time and was exhausted. She took an empty glass from the bedside table and went to get some water. But as she walked across the landing, she heard a noise and became frightened. What had happened that afternoon pursued her, taking away the temperance she usually had. She went to the living room and saw her father, a bottle of gin in his hand, wandering like a soul in torment. Without noticing her presence, he tried to take a sip, but as he bent to drink, he lost his balance and fell into a sitting position. He was so drunk he tried to grab the shadow of the bottle, which had come out of his hand when he'd fallen. Carmucha felt desolate. Her father carried on trying to grab that shadow several times, as if he was a robot bumping into a mirror. She opened her mouth to say something, but her eyes filled with tears again and drowned out her words. She ran back to her bedroom and got under the sheets, crying like a little baby. She wept as if she wished to soak the sheets, burying her head beneath the pillow, so she could shout out her pain lying in a pool of lament without being heard.

Early the next morning, she went to change the withered bunch of flowers at her mother's grave and for the first time in a long time didn't know what to say to her. She just rubbed furiously at the golden letters as if by doing this she might wipe out all the suffering in the world.

The girl is indignant. She writhes on the sofa as if she felt the pain Carmucha had felt.

'Poor thing.'

The old man sighs and nods mutely. He leans back in his chair. He seems emotional. Those recollections must bring very strong winds to his memory. His eyes struggle not to get wet. The tick-tock of the wall clock makes itself heard. The clouds open and sunlight assaults the house, crossing the windows without breaking or staining them, but warming them gently.

'But I don't understand,' says the girl.

'What is it you don't understand?'

'I don't understand anything, Grandpa. How could Carmucha calculate that shitty man's reaction so badly?' The girl's analytical character pleases the old man.

'Because everybody makes mistakes, even the cleverest people put their foot in it from time to time, but also because being homosexual back then was a terrible thing. You could go to jail for that.'

'Really?' The girl can't believe it. She opens her eyes as wide as two bowls of stars soup. The world her grandfather talks about seems as ancient as that of the pharaohs. The clock strikes the quarter hour and, by chance, produces the same little tune that used to be played in the living room of Carmucha's house.

'Until very recently civil guards were expelled if they were discovered to be homosexual. It would have been a disaster for him if they'd found out.'

The girl shakes her head, but carries on thinking.

'But back then, if he was gay, why…?' She doubts over her words. She looks down, full of confusion, not daring to finish her sentence, but there's no need for her to articulate the question because her grandfather comprehends her embarrassment and comes to her aid.

'Often rape doesn't have much to do with sex, it's just a way of abusing one's power, of showing the other they are at the rapist's mercy.' The old man watches as the girl clenches her teeth.

'But you can do that by beating somebody.'

'Yes, but it's not so humiliating. Also, in this case, it was a question of his virility. Yellow wanted to show she was completely wrong about him. He wanted to convince her there wasn't a tiny crack she could escape through, because he would be able to slip through it as well.' The old man purses his lips, aware of the double meaning contained in the game of words.

'But Grandpa! How can you joke about this? You adults are repulsive!' The girl hides her face with a cushion to cover her red cheeks.

'Some more than others, Marica.' The old man laughs at his own childish ability to be naughty. 'Trouble is you're just like her. Everything to do with sex strikes you as depraved.' The girl uncovers herself. She also smiles, looking at him with eyes full of camaraderie. 'But sex is also related to love and the survival instinct, don't you agree?' The old man winks at her, but she again covers her face with a gesture of disgust.

'Listen, Grandpa, stop being so disgusting and carry on with the story.'

The blow she had received from Yellow left her even more introverted than before. She almost always walked at top speed, worried about a possible betrayal and determined to find new ways of obtaining ever larger quantities of that black stone that drove everybody crazy. One day she was bustling along like always, staring at the ground, when she saw a child that was two or three years old next to a poor woman sitting on the pavement. They were begging near a church. It seemed to her the child was lying just a little bit too quietly for her to carry on. It's immediately obvious when little children are hungry, because not having any petrol to burn, they become less fidgety. She stopped to give the mother a few pesetas and, just as she was offering to take the child in while the mother begged, she saw Colin hurrying into the church.

When she'd finished talking to the woman, she went after Colin. She entered the nave with its smell of incense, walking cautiously. She was very careful because she didn't want to be discovered by the Englishman. She didn't want him to think she had a personal interest in him. But, to her surprise, she found the church was empty. Her head at once began to fill with doubts, suspicions, complots, extraordinary confabulations. Her thoughts, however, were interrupted by the sound of a door in the confessional. Behind the squeaking sound came Colin, who headed for the exit, making the sign of the cross like any parishioner. Carmucha hid behind a column, convinced this wasn't normal. There was no reason for the Englishman to be in a Catholic church. For a moment, she was afraid he was a double agent or might even be selling wolfram to the Germans with the priest as an intermediary.

Colin left the church immediately. Carmucha followed him for a couple of streets, but seeing his behaviour was now completely normal, she decided to call him. He turned around, narrowing his eyes a little, I think he was a bit short-sighted, and saw her gesturing to him. The Englishman looked to the left and to the right as if he didn't know her from Adam. It was the hour of the siesta and the street was empty. Carmucha went up to him.

'Do you have another consignment ready?' he asked in surprise, because she had only just delivered the previous one.

'It's not that,' she didn't bother putting a varnish on her agitated state. 'Are you Catholic?' she asked straight out, talking quickly as if she was in a hurry to reach the end of the interrogation.

The first time he'd seen her, Colin had thought she was a spoiled child, a snob who had taken an interest in wolfram as she might have done in opera. But in time he had begun to understand her and to like her. Some of her outbursts still struck him as naive, but he put up with them because he liked the girl. That day, he quashed her inquisitive tone with a big smile and one of the sweets he received from England. They were much nicer than the ones you could get here and he always used them to put a smile on the faces of the children he bumped into. She captured the message and smiled as well.

'Do you fancy a walk?' asked Colin when Carmucha had taken a sweet.

'I never go walking with Catholics.' She could be ingenious when she wanted.

'My father's a Protestant.' Colin accompanied his words with a gallant gesture, offering his company, and started walking. Carmucha followed him.

'I saw you coming out of a confessional.'

Colin shrugged his shoulders, avoiding the subject. He was trying to keep the tone light and make her forget she was in a hurry.

'I'm glad I met you because I have some very good news.' He saw with a quick glance that she was still engrossed in the subject he wanted to avoid, but carried on regardless. 'From now on, I shall pay three hundred a kilo.'

She didn't like him changing the subject like that and stopped in the middle of the pavement. His attempt to avoid giving an answer had aroused her suspicions once again.

It looked like it might rain, but the summer wasn't prepared to give up the ghost quite yet. The clouds were incapable of releasing their cargo, all they did was create a sultry atmosphere that set everybody on edge.

'What were you doing in the church?'

'Oh, nothing. It's not important.'

'Answer the question or I'll go and ask the priest.'

Colin huffed, but remained silent, looking at her like a father tired of fighting with his daughter. Carmucha turned around and headed back towards the church. Colin thought her shoes made a really lovely sound as they collided with the paving stones.

'I went to give him some money.'

Colin's words stopped Carmucha, who turned around and stared at him uncomprehendingly. A peal of thunder reached them from far away, echoing in the mountains. Perhaps there it had started to rain already.

'Why?'

'Why are you always so nosy?' She didn't reply, quiet and stubborn like a small pedigree dog biting the bottoms of his trousers. A woman ran by. She must have gone for a walk in her new dress, but forgotten to take an umbrella. 'The priest has a soup kitchen for local people in need. He feeds more and more people, and I help him. That's all.' He could have added he was doing the same as her with her women's school, but Carmucha had never talked about her initiative in the red-light district. Colin pretended not to know anything about her, though he'd done his research. Like a good spy, he preferred to show only one card, making out he was showing his whole hand.

'So why all the mystery?' she asked, happy to think the example of the women's school was spreading.

'Because I'm English, I'm Protestant… because I do what I do. The priest would have to give lots of explanations if he was asked about me.'

Carmucha thought he may not have been as selfish as she'd imagined.

'I thought you were a sceptic,' she remarked ironically.

'I don't trust organizations very much, but I do trust a few people.' He was embarrassed. He looked like a macho boy who's been caught crying. She, on the other hand, was enchanted. This was probably the closest she'd got to a gallant conversation in all her life.

'So you trust this priest?'

'This one, yes, he's not one of those lying, smarmy Francoists.'

The conversation took Colin by surprise because since the first time he'd seen her, however much he'd tried, he hadn't managed to talk to her about anything other than wolfram. Carmucha was comfortable because she felt she had the Englishman under control. She liked that sense of domination after the arrogance he'd displayed towards her at the start of their commercial relationship. But Colin wanted his own back as well, after the times she'd left him standing on the dance floor and all the other times he'd made an effort to be pleasant with her.

'How do you know? How can you be sure he's not one of those?' asked Carmucha with the air of a triumphant prosecutor.

'Because I met him in a brothel,' he said with all the ease in the world, looking up at the sky, which was beginning to release large, noisy drops.

Carmucha didn't like getting this taste of her own medicine, but pretended not to give it any importance, accepting the reply with a sporting gesture and smiling awkwardly.

'All right then, I'm off,' she said, but the facts contradicted her words. Her feet remained planted on the pavement as if they'd been trapped there by a net. The water started making her wet. A few drops ran down her forehead, sliding slowly down skin that was already dotted with sweat. 'Why are you upping the price if I haven't even asked you?'

'I have my reasons,' replied the Englishman, still savouring his revenge. He opened an umbrella he was carrying, but hadn't remembered until then, and offered her shelter.

Carmucha thought this was beginning to resemble a game of poker she didn't much feel like playing, so, in confirmation of what she'd just said, she shrugged her shoulders and left.

The Englishman was sorry to have broken that string she had agreed to pull on for the first time, but it was too late. He stood there on the deserted pavement, hanging onto the umbrella beneath the rain, watching her retreat without looking back.

October arrived, and the storms, instead of quietening down, seemed to spread everywhere, like an infectious epidemic advancing through all aspects of life. Having bought that small, exhausted mine with an outlaw's methods, Carmucha and her team used it to store material and met there on a regular basis, as if it was their castle. One windy afternoon, coming out of the black cave that led into the earth, Félix wanted to tell her happily what he'd read in the papers: the British had just disembarked in Naples. Carmucha, however, didn't reply. She was annoyed because he'd arranged a deal on his own. The deal consisted in talking to some employees about stealing six wagons full of mineral from the Germans' mines. The idea wasn't very original. It was a question of going in through the breathing holes, hanging off ropes down to the galleries, and taking the wolfram the miners had left in the prearranged place. I say it wasn't very original because lots of seekers went in through breathing holes, but they did so on the off chance – to see what they could find – and normally only came across empty galleries. Besides, it was usual for them to get hurt as they were going up or down the narrow ventilation shafts. Félix had gone a step further, talking to some of his old colleagues and offering them lots of money in return for their collaboration. Carmucha, however, didn't like the way he'd gone and done all this without asking her. She was very worried and full of foreboding. What with one thing and another, she had this dizzy sensation, as if a whirlpool was opening up in ground that had always struck her as solid and secure. She was nervous and grumpy like a deaf old woman.

That night, once they were on the mountain, she cursed the clouds that kept on passing by. She thought the moon was shining far too brightly. She saw Pepiño and Moncho's shadows advancing and disappearing into a hole dug in the earth and looked into the distance, where the lights of the mine twinkled in the darkness. No movement could be seen. The wind had died down and the night wasn't cold. She heard a little owl call. Everything seemed calm, but she just couldn't settle down. Then she heard a noise and looked around. Another shadow appeared from behind a bramble bush.

'Change that expression, woman. The wolfram's where we discussed. Six wagons full,' Félix whispered so he wouldn't be heard by the guards.

'And the breathing hole?' she also talked softly.

'It's fine. Very wide. With ropes, you can get down easily.'

He disappeared back into the darkness, and Carmucha advanced towards the hole her men had gone down. Pepiño of Setes was holding onto a rope, waiting for the tug that indicated the first sack was ready to be brought up. After a few long seconds, she saw the rope going down, being pulled from Pepiño's hands into the depths of the earth. The young man smiled at Carmucha and started pulling with all his might. There was then the sound of branches breaking and Félix leaped out, making fun of his boss' nervous gesture. He grabbed his colleague's rope silently and with rhythmic movements, like sailors rowing, they raised the wolfram in a moment. Pepiño threw the sack over his shoulder and left. Félix dropped the rope back down the hole.

Carmucha went on the lookout again. She thought she could see something next to the mine's buildings, as if a light had started moving. She became alert, warning Félix with a tap on the shoulder.

'Don't worry, it's a guard. They don't normally come this way.'

The tone of his murmurs was confident and soothing, but the light carried on moving and seemed to draw closer.

'What do you mean by normally?' Félix didn't know how to reply. 'How much did you pay him?' continued Carmucha.

'What the hell am I going to pay that lot for? They never come this way,' Félix gesticulated nervously, trying to justify himself in his off-hand manner, but even in the darkness he could see in the girl's eyes two cauldrons surrounded by fire, with a man just like him cooking in the boiling water. Carmucha had turned into the queen of bandits.

'Money is the only universal language, Félix.' She chewed her words and spat them in his face. 'You have to pay everybody! Always!'

'He'll turn around, you'll see.' The two of them waited, watching the torch, which continued advancing. 'Besides, I never liked this lot. They're not like workers. They defend the company as if it was theirs...' He lost the thread when he saw the torch drawing closer and left his sentence unfinished. He felt terribly awkward, recalling his words when Carmucha had said he shouldn't make deals without talking to her first. He had replied he wasn't a child and could look after himself without the need for a nursemaid. At that moment, he felt very much like a child, like a snotty-nosed idiot. When he heard the footsteps of Pepiño, who was coming back after taking away the sack, he gestured nervously to him to hide. Pepiño slipped into the shadows in absolute silence.

But the light of the torch carried on advancing.

Félix cursed under his breath.

'Come,' he said to Carmucha. 'We can hide in the breathing hole.'

'So we get caught like rabbits?' Carmucha was furious. Félix didn't know what to do. The light was so close they could discern the guard's outline.

'How much do guards earn?' she asked.

'Fifteen pesetas a day.'

She gave him another iron look and advanced towards the light without replying, walking close to the ground, almost on all fours.

The guard must have heard some kind of noise and continued moving towards the breathing hole. He wasn't all that confident and walked cautiously, lighting the brambles with his torch every time he noticed something strange. When Carmucha had him very close, she used one of his pauses to stand up without being seen. The guard surveyed the area in front of him, moving the torch as if it was a lighthouse, and discovered her with her arms up. She had a wad of notes in one hand and was moving them so he could see them. The man kept the torch on Carmucha, who slowly brought the hand that was free to her face and placed her forefinger on her lips.

'Can you lower the torch? You can see I'm unarmed.' The guard obeyed. 'I have to ask a favour.' She spoke in the dulcet tones of a goody two-shoes. 'I want you to go back to the mine and forget you ever saw me. If you do that, you can take these ten thousand pesetas.'

The guard remained silent. Carmucha couldn't see his face. It was just a black silhouette that might have been thinking about everything it could do with ten thousand pesetas or about the best way to catch her. If he didn't accept the deal, they would end up being reported, arrested and put in court. Or, worse still, they would end up in Yellow's clutches.

'Leave the money on the ground and go back ten paces.' The guard spoke with the seseo used in Carnota and places like that. Carmucha obeyed. The man's silhouette approached the money and stuffed the notes in his pockets with the speed of a hoover. But instead of leaving as she'd asked, he again pointed the torch at her. Carmucha thought she was lost. She reckoned the guard was planning to keep the money and to report her.

'If you don't betray me, I can come back more often,' she said in desperation.

'My name's Moaña. You can find me in the bar Paris in Noia.' The guard rotated the torch to illuminate his own face. So she would recognize him. He was cross-eyed like a weathervane. He switched off the light. Carmucha heard the sound of his footsteps retreating in the tranquillity of the night.

Even though it didn't arrive suddenly, like the summer of some film or theatre performance or whatever, people began to suspect this could be the last winter, the last winter with joy, excess and easy money, money earned here with ease thanks to the tragedy of those killing each other in the war in Europe.

The winter passed in a frenzy.

The British and Americans were advancing in Italy, and there were rumours about an imminent allied landing somewhere in Europe. They sounded like old wives' tales, like the ones told earlier about the possibilities of defeating the German army, but doubts quickly increased.

Carmucha didn't let a business deal slip by. She carried on taking wolfram from the mine and buying in Roxelio's bar. She also acquired material directly on the mountain, when some miner came across a good vein and sold her the whole lot. Then Félix's men would grab a pick and shovel and extract the wolfram themselves. There were nine of them now. They formed the strongest and most highly respected team on the mountain. Nobody picked a fight with them and even the Civil Guard left them alone. From time to time, the guards would stop another gang, warm their backs and, having given them a good hiding, suggest they might want to pay more if they didn't want to get a nasty surprise. But Félix's team got through the winter without any problems.

The women's school also functioned without difficulties. At that time, the police would come to receive a commission wherever there were prostitutes and to hand out a couple of slaps whenever there was any kind of subversion. But in the case of the women's school they preferred to pretend they didn't know the place existed in exchange for a few pesetas. That was pretty extraordinary because the intention in that place was to alter in a clearly subversive way what old right-wingers with their local-boss attitude are in the habit of calling 'the natural order of things'. Carmucha felt stronger all the time and thought deep down, in spite of appearances, Yellow was afraid of her. She thought she'd paid a toll, but in exchange for the outrage she'd been subjected to, she'd earned the privileged situation she was now in.

It was in the school where Carmucha felt calmest. One day she went up to Coñoño and put the money she gave him for his help in his pocket. The boy was messing around with some children. Apparently it was amazing to see how well he got on with all of them. As Carmucha left the room, he went after her, wanting to give her back the money. He said he also wanted to learn to read and, if she taught him like another prostitute, she wouldn't have to pay him. Coñoño was half stupid, but had a sense of humour. Carmucha was delighted. It was that kind of thing that made her happy. Of course, she didn't want the money back and carried on paying him as well as teaching him to read.

She then bought a car, her own car. It was a black Citroën like a thoroughbred, with this long snout and mudguards that were round like the headlights they supported. It was a wonder. You wouldn't believe how she drove. Not because she went really fast, as young people do nowadays, but because after only three days of having the car she drove incredibly smoothly. It was as if she'd been born for this. You didn't even notice when she changed gear.

Around March, one day she arrived late, as almost always happened after she got the car, she did something strange. I think she was undergoing an internal struggle. On the one hand, she still had her obsession for independence, for a woman's personal autonomy, but her feminine nature was demanding things she didn't know where to include in her lifestyle. The truth is this episode hurt Félix a great deal.

The weather had improved enormously and people were using this opportunity to go to the mountain because there wasn't so much mud and it was easier to work. As a result, wolfram was pouring into the marketeers' stores and throats were getting dry. So, what with one thing and another, Roxelio's bar was like an anthill. One of those days, Félix noticed Carmucha was distracted. She was weighing a miner's mineral, but didn't seem to be inside her body, as if she was on one of her outings, which she alternated between the horse and the car. He approached her ear and whispered in his off-hand manner:

'I hear six bombs fell on the Vatican and the Pope is up in arms.'

Carmucha ignored this remark. She counted out a hundred and ninety-five pesetas and gave them to the miner. The man shook hands and left.

'You know what they say about you?' said Félix in a whisper again. Another miner came to occupy the place the previous one had vacated. Carmucha gestured to him to wait while she heard what Félix had to say. 'They say you don't like men.' She smiled impishly and stared into his eyes.

'And what do you think?'

Félix escaped her look by pretending to scour her body with a dealer's eyes. Carmucha was wearing the kind of suit she always put on when she was after wolfram. She looked like one of those English explorers from the start of the twentieth century and it suited her perfectly.

'I can't imagine you being married,' lied Félix in a whisper.

'Do you want to accompany me to the dance?' she replied in the same tone. 'If I go with a man, perhaps they'll stop calling me a butch.'

Félix was stunned. What was he going to do among all those gentlemen in the Casino? He had no manners and didn't know how to associate with such people.

'Me?' She nodded with a coquettish smile. 'But I…'

'Are you coming or not?' she insisted, ignoring his doubts and gesturing to the miner to sit down.

Félix quickly said yes before the opportunity vanished and ran to the bar for a glass of liquor – to clear his head, so he said.

The Casino was heaving that evening. Félix combed his hair back with some gel he bought at a chemist's in Noia and put on his Sunday best, the same he'd worn at Manuela's funeral. He didn't spend money as if it burned his hands, like lots of other people, and still had more or less the same clothes he'd had when he came back from the war. But that evening he was beside himself. When he entered the Casino with Carmucha on his arm, dressed in her mother's clothes, he thought the two of them made a Hollywood couple. He noticed people looking at him with curiosity and envy. He was taking Carmucha to the dance! Who ever would have thought it! They had a couple of drinks and talked a lot. The atmosphere in that large hall was so extraordinary the chandeliers trembled by themselves, as if there was an earthquake, or at least that's what he thought. He told stories he'd never told before, some of them very dirty, and the two of them fell about laughing. They caused such an uproar that they attracted people's attention. In effect, the manners of that place were not the ones Félix was used to, but Carmucha, instead of introducing him to the Casino's formal style, went along with it and encouraged him to be eccentric. She ordered glasses of liquor and drank them down in one, banging them on the counter, the way they did in the bar of Roxelio of the priest.

Matías was at a table with Don Severo. The two of them viewed this coarse behaviour with disapproval. Carmucha acted innocently, but kept her eyes open. She wasn't so worried about her father as about Colin, who was flirting with a local girl.

Félix asked if she wanted to dance and, when she accepted, headed off so proudly he accidentally knocked over the glass of a high-society lady. The girl's new dress was covered in wine and she was indignant. She said that's what happened to people who didn't know how to behave themselves. Carmucha was offended by this remark, so, in order to annoy her, she took out a note and stuffed it down her cleavage, as if they were at Rita's. The young man with her said this was an intolerable insult and flirted with the idea of getting uppity. But one look from Félix and a couple of words in his ear made him reconsider his attitude. He paled slightly and took the girl to the toilets to help her wash and, above all, to calm her nerves.

Matías and the mayor watched this episode from a distance. Don Severo turned to Matías, inviting him to intervene.

Carmucha and Félix immediately took possession of the dance floor. They moved with the free, wild energy of the mountain, which in the heart of the town's social system seemed violent and threatening. Colin, however, accepted the challenge and joined them, entering the dance floor with the girl he was flirting with. He immediately made a gesture, suggesting a change of partner. The women changed hands, but the dance didn't die down. The four of them carried on twisting and turning like a whirlpool.

Matías watched from the edge of the dance floor.

Carmucha, laughing as she hadn't laughed in years, went back from Colin's hands to Félix's. People gathered to view the spectacle. Carmucha was happy. She remembered when she was a girl and went on the carousel that was set up on the fairground during the festivities. Then, like now, at each turn she would pass next to her father, who kept an eye on her. That night, however he wasn't smiling as when he saw her on a golden wooden horse, instead he looked worried. Carmucha excused herself and went over to Matías.

'Don't you think you've had enough?' asked her father with a false smile. Now that really was an injustice. The first time he'd seen her enjoy herself and laugh like a little child, he should have been more understanding, but all he ever saw was the social sacrilege.

'Look who's talking,' said Carmucha and headed to the toilets.

She went to the basin and wet her face to clear her thoughts. She was sweating like a horse. She looked in the mirror, fanning herself with her hands, and saw Colin reflected in the glass. The Englishman looked at her with a gesture of ironic disapproval.

'It seems the tables have turned.' Carmucha shrugged her shoulders. 'Now you're the one who's drinking to forget.'

'No, I'm drinking because I don't have anything better to do.' As she talked, she gathered her hair in a reflex movement.

'I thought you had aims, you were fighting for a cause.'

Carmucha headed towards the door, but since he didn't move aside to let her pass, she stopped on the threshold. Their faces were only a couple of inches apart.

'Well, you're mistaken. I'm just trying to escape this wretched world.'

'You were more attractive when serene.'

'And you were more amusing when you'd been drinking.'

Colin tried to get closer, but she stepped past him and escaped down the corridor.

When she reached the bar, her glass was waiting for her where she'd left it before going to dance. She drank it down in one. Colin came up behind her.

'Tomorrow a boat with wolfram is leaving for England. Would you like to come with me to supervise the cargo?'

Carmucha turned her head. She wanted to say no, but she fancied going. She was curious to see the departure of illegal goods. She wanted to see it with her own eyes because apparently none of that existed. She was starting to wonder whether in fact all that extraordinary business of the wolfram wasn't a complete sham. Colin took advantage of her indecision to order another round.

Félix watched the scene, sweating at his table, clinging to a glass of brandy as shipwrecked sailors might cling to a life belt. He saw them talking, slowly lifting their glasses off the bar, behaving like two high-society people, and felt his unconfessed hopes vanishing as they came into contact with reality, a reality as wild as his mountain manners. He saw them look at each other, clink glasses in a toast, and heard very clearly the high-pitched sound, that slight sound that travels a great distance, the sound that is made when two glasses come together and a heart breaks.

The night was as dark and silent as an act of betrayal. Some sleepy seagulls gazed bad-temperedly at the yellow light and let out an unintelligible complaint. Colin had just opened the office door and the glow of the filament inside a naked bulb had hurt their eyes. With much more curiosity than the seagulls, Carmucha was waiting in front of the small hut, observing the tiny two-storey building, which seemed to merge with the night. Upstairs was the office lit by a single wretched bulb and downstairs the storehouse full of odds and ends. Colin descended the wooden stairs slowly, holding a piece of paper covered in official seals, which he waved in the air as he came up to her.

'Coal destined for Oslo. Authorized to weigh anchor at once,' he said with a mocking smile.

They started walking silently towards the quay. Colin was listening to the sound of Carmucha's shoes colliding with the paving stones and didn't hear the detonations in the distance very well.

'Is there a festivity?' she asked.

'As far as I understand, once spring arrives, there's always some kind of festivity going on.' Carmucha accepted this answer, but it was March and spring had yet to arrive.

Two men appeared behind the storehouse, ran past them like a pair of greyhounds and immediately vanished into the darkness, heading in the direction of the offices. Another detonation, louder and sharper than before, sounded in the distance. Then a lighter one. Carmucha looked for an answer in Colin's eyes, but he was scanning the sky, where the only extraordinary thing Carmucha could see was the Milky Way pointing towards Compostela.

Some lights appeared at the far end of the quay, heading towards them. Carmucha started feeling uneasy. It was a truck that stopped when it reached them. The driver was a fat man with a moustache and a cap covered in grime.

'Everything's ready. They're just waiting for the papers to weigh anchor,' he said to Colin, his face lit up with satisfaction.

The Englishman, however, had lost the sense of humour he'd shown when coming down from the office. He jumped onto the running board of the truck and handed the driver the safe-conduct.

'Give this to the captain and tell him to leave at once. Got it?'

The driver took the piece of paper and, as soon as Colin had jumped back down, started turning around. Carmucha approached, unclear why he was suddenly in such a hurry.

'What's going on?' she asked, gazing at the horizon, the place the Englishman kept looking at. At that moment, there came, rolling across the dark waters, the peal of another detonation.

'I think we're attacking a submarine.'

Carmucha was paralyzed and stared at him as if he'd gone mad. A light illuminated the sky, like an enormous firework, and this time the sound arrived very quickly, almost immediately after the flash. Colin grabbed her arm and pulled her into the shelter of the closest shed.

'Have you heard of the Battle of the Atlantic?'

'Yes, but I didn't think it reached…' She realized she was hiding next to a shed in a port on the Atlantic Ocean and didn't continue.

'The air force chases German submarines to their harbours. Sometimes right here. A few months ago, they sank one in Ortigueira Bay.'

'But if…' Carmucha was astonished. She couldn't understand how the war could be taking place right there and nobody knew about it. The muffled sound of hardworking engines could be heard in the night.

'I know they never say anything about it in the press, but it's true,' Colin pointed towards the sea, holding out his arm. 'Look!'

Carmucha saw a very white circular stain advancing at top speed, sweeping the surface of the waters as if a flying plate were ploughing the bay, sending down a stream of light. Having advanced across the sea, the circle rushed towards the land. The light scoured the quay, making the storehouses, boats, nets and piles of fish traps suddenly visible, with the clarity of day. Carmucha watched in ecstasy as the light approached her, illuminating that abruptly magical scene and submerging everything it left behind in darkness. She lifted her head and saw an enormous-looking seaplane passing over her. On its fuselage, the aircraft had a set of lights pointing at the ground. The roar of the engines was frightful. Having passed over them, the aircraft turned around.

'It's an American seaplane,' said Colin, shouting in her ear. 'They're going to attack again.'

The plane returned to the horizon, but this time it flew over the bay, re-opening a path of light on the waters, which turned green beneath it. As the plane moved away, they realized the truck was coming back. Colin went to meet it.

'They're leaving now,' shouted the driver without stopping, slowing down before accelerating again in order to get out of there as quickly as possible.

Colin did a thumbs-up and went back to Carmucha.

'It's better to go. There are people coming I would prefer not to meet.' The Englishman's words were followed by another boom in the distance. Colin looked at her, indicating which way to go with his outstretched arm, waiting for her to leave so he could go after her, but the girl didn't move.

'Why don't we hide and see what happens?' she asked mischievously.

Colin sighed. He didn't fancy staying there, but wanted to please her. He gestured to her to follow and headed for the sheds in search of shelter. The sliding doors were unlocked. They pushed one on its rail and went in.

The port fell into silence. The war seemed to have vanished in the night, like a mirage. Carmucha looked out through the openings in the wood. She was quiet for a while, observing the calm. She was fascinated by the way the war could come and go. She thought about the way it arrived, destroying everything like an iron broom that sweeps life before it, with no time to think, those affected by the disaster unable to understand what's happening to them.

'My mother was English as well, you know?'

Colin knew this, but was curious to learn the details and, above all, to get to know Carmucha.

'Oh, yes? Where from?' he asked with fake surprise.

'She was born in Manchester, but ever since she was a girl she spent her summers in San Sebastián. That was where she met my father.'

'Did she die?' he inquired as if he was uncertain.

She nodded sadly.

'She was a schoolteacher. At the start of the civil war, she was forced to stop teaching. Nobody stood up for her and little by little she ebbed away until she died of sorrow,' Carmucha couldn't help getting emotional when talking about her mother.

Colin was moved by her words. He wanted to hug her to give her some consolation, but limited himself to putting a hand on her waist. She jerked away as if she'd received an electric shock and took a step backwards, rejecting all contact.

'Let's go,' she said, as if asking for help. 'There's nothing happening here.'

Outside, they heard some voices. They peered through the gaps. Several plain-clothed sailors were with a group of men dressed in German navy uniform. Most of their clothes were soaked; some of them, slightly wounded, walked with difficulty, leaning on a companion.

'Germans!' exclaimed Carmucha in a whisper still weighed down with incredulity.

'It seems we sank the submarine. They'll take them to Ferrol, to the *Max Albrecht*, the supply ship. They'll see to them there and make them better. Then they'll send them back to Germany so they can carry on trying to kill us,' Colin couldn't avoid a sense of bitterness at the false neutrality of Franco's government.

Some of the soldiers were very young, practically children, glancing around with frightened faces. One of them knelt down and kissed the ground, glad to be back on dry land. He then went to hug the sailors who had rescued them; the sailors smiled, happy to have saved the lives of these poor men.

'There's a German supply ship in Ferrol?' asked Carmucha in amazement, as the group of Germans disappeared into the darkness of the port.

'Yes, and in Vigo there's another, the *Bessel*. Sometimes they repair the submarines that have been damaged by our attacks, or they fill them with petrol.' She listened to his explanations, open-mouthed. 'They also have a radio transmitter in Cospeito. It's called Elektra Sonne. They use it to determine their exact position at sea. We were thinking of sabotaging it, but then we understood it could help us as well.' He fell silent for a moment, as if he thought he'd said too much. 'The German consul will arrive soon and he'll probably be accompanied by some important Falangist. It would be better to leave.'

Carmucha was so impressed by this news that she followed him without asking any more questions, like an obedient, frightened child.

I think the events Carmucha lived through in the final months of '43 and the first months of '44 caused her to lose touch with reality a little. To her, the world was nothing more now than a heap of lies, piled one on top of the other, in an indecipherable skein. The only certainty she had left was her determination to confront it with all her strength. Every day that went by, the fame of her team and the small legends about her courage increased, making her a popular heroine who stood up for the miners against the oppressive force of Yellow and his men. Since there was no justice, there was a wish to find some hope, even if that hope landed on the shoulders of a poor girl who had to carry the enormous weight of becoming a mythological heroine. Little by little, she began to believe she was that heroic figure people talked about in the taverns.

One hot afternoon, Pepiño of Setes and Moncho Rañal learned that the period without problems with the Civil Guard had come to an end. They were tying a few sacks of wolfram they had just hauled onto the horses' saddles, chatting to the miners who'd discovered the vein, when the silhouettes of some civil guards appeared from behind a hill that crowned the ridge they were working on. The guards' shadows fell on top of them. Seeing they were none too friendly, Pepiño and Moncho tried to mount the horses and gallop off, but some other guards came from the sides and stopped them. The corporal in charge asked to see their permit for transporting wolfram. What this amounted to was a declaration of war because nobody transported mineral with a permit, except for the Germans and the guards when they were about their own business. Pepiño replied he had permission from Yellow, but this declaration, which wasn't entirely false, earned him a blow from the butt of a rifle that broke two of his teeth.

'Don't lie, you bastard. Don't lie, otherwise things could get worse,' said the guard, taking the horse's reins as if the horse belonged to him.

'Whatever you take from me, Carmucha will take from you with interest,' cried Pepiño from the ground, spitting the blood out of his mouth. The guard started kicking him so he would shut up, but then Moncho spoke.

'Carmucha's not afraid of you.' Another blow with the butt of the rifle rendered him unconscious.

The miners watched in silence, but without lowering their heads. The guards, despite being protected by their uniforms, aimed at them in fear.

'Carmucha will punish you,' said a voice behind the corporal. The guard turned to see where the voice had come from, but everybody there was quiet.

'Carmucha's not afraid of you!' shouted another anonymous throat, behind him again. He turned around once more, but discovered nothing. More voices were raised. Everybody declared that Carmucha would avenge them. The boss gestured and the guards left, taking the wolfram in the saddlebags and fear in their bodies.

The consequences of that attack were not long coming. Carmucha carried on investing in the purchase of wills and paid large bribes to a lot of people. She had even bought off the odd guard who had an account to settle with Yellow, which enabled her to have the best possible information as to his movements.

It was on a bendy road, almost buried among the trees, which twisted and turned in the direction of Lousame mine. They saw the truck approach as it turned a corner and stood in the middle of the road, waiting for it to arrive. The driver was half distracted, singing 'La Bien Pagá', and turning the steering wheel with the energy that road required. When he saw the two hooded figures aiming at him with their pistols, he slammed on the brakes. The roll-up he was smoking fell out of his lips. The wheels skidded on the tarmac and the truck came to a halt, mixing the smell of petrol with that of burned rubber. The driver rummaged about between his legs, trying to get rid of the cigarette, which was burning his trousers and threatening to pass through them and scorch his skin. The hooded figures, who were in fact Carmucha and Félix, ran to the cabin. Félix opened the door while she aimed with her pistol. Pepiño, Moncho and the others came out of their hiding place, leading two horse-drawn carts.

'Out of the truck!' shouted Félix.

The driver obeyed. Carmucha went to have a look at the cargo. Pepiño and the others started transferring the wolfram from the truck to the carts.

'Don't shoot, please don't shoot,' cried the driver, who was trembling with fear. He put his hands on his head, pushing back the greasy locks that hid his bald patch.

'Quieten down, for fuck's sake!' ordered Félix. The man was so nervous he didn't stop jumping about. He lowered his hands and put them on his thighs. His blue work overalls were more covered in shit than the perch in a chicken coop.

'Get your hands out of your pockets! Do you want this to end badly, or what the hell is wrong with you?' Félix was indignant. He thought it was going to be very difficult to carry out a clean job with a guy like this, and he was right. The driver moved his hands from his pockets, but started walking backwards. His teeth were chattering like war drums.

'Where the hell are you going?' Félix lowered his pistol to see if the man would quieten down, but even that didn't work. The poor wretch carried on backtracking without looking where he was going and, having bumped into the barrier that protected the road from the gully, fell into the void.

'The guy's an idiot!' Félix ran to the barrier and looked down. Carmucha came up beside him. The driver was spreadeagled in the gorse. At the end of the day, he'd been lucky. He'd fallen from a height of eight metres – the normal thing would have been to break his neck, but he was in a pretty good state. He kept complaining, but he was moving and there was nothing seriously wrong, except for a broken leg.

'What the hell are you doing, you fool! What are you doing? Quieten down, won't you?' Félix felt like giving him a good hiding because of the lack of professionalism he'd shown.

'We'll have to get him out of there,' said Carmucha before turning back to the truck. 'Come on, let's transfer the cargo as quickly as we can.'

'But we're not to blame, you got that? Don't even think about saying any different, otherwise you can stay there,' Félix addressed the driver, who was far too worried about his pains to understand what was being said.

That same afternoon, Carmucha went to the women's school just like any other day. The crazier she was about her exploits as the queen of bandits, the more she needed the calm of the classes. There, she behaved like another teacher, although some of the sentences she wrote on the board for her pupils to copy down betrayed her feelings. That afternoon, she wrote, 'Every pig gets its St Martin,' and placed the chalk on the desk with a smile on her lips.

'Right then, who can read this sentence?'

Coñoño's hand shot up as if he wanted to touch the ceiling. Carmucha was surprised and gave him permission. The boy still had lots of difficulty reading and had never volunteered before.

'Every pig gets its St Mar-tin,' he said with difficulty, but lots of determination.

'Not bad for a little madam,' remarked the Ourensan, patting him on the back. 'And we thought he was stupid. You sure learned to read, didn't you? You bastard!'

The other prostitutes also celebrated the boy's heroics with their rude language, patting him and giving him the odd innocent kiss. Carmucha observed the fruits of her work with satisfaction and Coñoño felt happy finally to have given an indication of his intelligence.

In the Casino, however, Carmucha's exploits did not go down well. Times were hard and fear was on the increase. The night seemed calm. The tables were busy and men were chatting. The murmur of low voices floated between them, carrying information and lies from group to group.

Don Rüdiger was playing cards at the poker table, where Tirín was as well, accompanied by other players. He was betting so high several men were watching the game. There was no talking. It was enough to see the luck hidden by the backs of cards and stony expressions. But advancing between the tables, listening to snippets of that conversation built out of the conversations of everybody, there could be heard a discourse that spoke of fear and hope; of fear of change and of hope; of fear of change and of hope there was still enough time to take advantage; of fear that the mirage of prosperity, of a comfortable life on an island on the margins of reality, might disappear, but at the same time of hope that the mirage might vanish after they had made enough money to live the rest of their lives out in ease. Voices criss-crossed in the air, turning into a single contradictory, but coherent discourse. One German complained of the impossibility of a single country dominating the whole world, but his complaints were mollified by the false, pleasant words of one of his clients. A drunk laughed at Franco's recent decision to drastically reduce sales of wolfram to Germany. He twisted his tongue, saying this was a useless consequence of the Americans' threat of an oil embargo if they didn't stop selling wolfram to the Germans. He laughed because he was sure, as was everybody, that the less mineral that made it to Germany on an official basis, the more would be smuggled out, and at a higher price. An Englishman, who was also pretty drunk, argued with a companion, saying the Germans intended to exterminate the Jews. His companion couldn't believe this, it seemed far too stupid an idea. The other replied if they'd been stupid enough to invade Russia in winter, they were capable of any kind of idiocy. The conversation continued at the table occupied by Don Severo and Matías. They were deeply concerned about their own affairs. Matías' face was as white as a sheet, but he endeavoured to cheer himself up by drinking some gin. The mayor was relating details about the heist on the truck.

'The wolfram was from Portugal. For him, it's very easy to get it across the border without problems and he can buy it there seven times cheaper than here. He then takes it to the mine and sells it to the Germans, who claim it as their own production.' Don Severo observed Matías in search of some sign that would give him away, but only saw him nodding and taking a swig from his gin. 'You can understand the profit margins are enormous. I don't suppose we have anything to do with this…' He gazed at him with the look of an indulgent judge, of an understanding, but seriously worried father.

'No, no. You can be sure of that,' replied Matías, staring into his gin.

'I say this because things are starting to get out of hand. I sometimes think we're on the verge of subversion.' Don Severo lit a cigarette and anxiously sucked in the smoke. He was sweating.

'So long as there's money coming in, the regime will put up with subversion.' Matías proposed a toast, trying to lighten the conversation, which was starting to head in a direction he preferred to avoid. Don Severo clicked his tongue and didn't respond to the toast.

'You can't go meddling in Yellow's business affairs because he'll start arresting people and complicating things, understand?' Matías nodded silently. The mayor was getting all worked up. 'Who could be so stupid as to do a thing like that?' Matías, as if he couldn't imagine such a madman could exist, pretended to wonder who could do such a crazy thing. 'I'm only saying this in case, but I'm worried about your daughter. I heard tell she's turning into a kind of heroine for the miners. This is going too far. She's a woman, Matías. We can't allow the Civil Guard to be made to look ridiculous. What respect will the guards impose if a silly little girl can mess around with them and get away with it?' He grabbed his cigarette. He looked like he was going to gobble it down. Matías no longer had the strength to raise his glass.

'Don't worry. She's only a girl and…' He looked at Severo, who was huffing and puffing like the Rías Altas train. 'I'll talk to her…' Don Severo nodded.

They were silent for a time before changing subject.

Matías got up early the next morning. He had to go to the bank first thing and, by the time the office opened, he was waiting already. When he got home, he went to knock at the door of Carmucha's room. When he got no answer, he went in, thinking she must still be asleep. But the bed was empty. There was more order in that room than in the cell of the strictest prison. The bed was made and slippers were placed under the bedside table, at an equal distance from each of the legs. On the dressing table, everything seemed to have been fixed in its position and even the photograph of Katharine Hepburn had found its place in a corner symmetrically opposite the portrait of her mother. She had given it a similar frame. It even had a dedication, and yet the signature was not an artist's, but Rebeca's. He was about to close the door when he noticed the bedspread had a strange fold on the pillow. Before going out, he went to tidy the bedspread, but discovered something that made his blood run cold.

Under the pillow, there was a pistol.

Milagros finished serving Carmucha. Matías, who was watching her movements, smiled when she looked at him, awaiting his instructions.

'Thank you, Milagros. Everything is fine.'

The maid left.

Carmucha started tucking into her food. However, when she saw her father wasn't eating, but watching her with a sad expression, she also stopped eating. The two of them were silent for a few moments. She mistook the pain in her father's eyes for the glimmer of a rebuke and looked at him haughtily.

'You can't always win, you know?' said Matías.

'What makes you say that? Is there some kind of problem?'

Matías passed his hand over his forehead, combing back his hair. He didn't want Carmucha to see the conversation as an argument, because then she wouldn't accept the facts and would twist the conclusions.

'I'm worried you don't realize what you're doing.'

'I do the same as everybody else,' she answered, sticking the fork in her mouth.

'You do the same as those who've always gone hungry. Those who have something don't risk everything for a handful of coins.' Matías spoke softly, almost sweetly, but she replied with mountain brutality.

'And what did I have, Papa?' She carried on eating without looking at him. Matías, meanwhile, refused to be budged by that insinuation.

'There are invincible things, Carmucha. Sometimes, the complications are too great, it's better to take a step back, because if you don't, they may finish you off.' He was going to continue talking, but Carmucha got there first, incapable of putting up with a discourse that struck her as so hypocritical.

'That's right! That's always been your philosophy, that's why you didn't try to help Mother when she was forbidden to teach. That's why she got ill! That's why she died of sorrow, Papa!' She had started to shout, but on realizing this, she endeavoured to lower her tone. 'She died because she couldn't bear the fact her husband didn't fight to defend her. See how you hobnob with your high-society friends! Why didn't you do that when she needed it?'

Matías took a deep breath. He was about to get emotional and was afraid he wouldn't be able to carry on talking, but he swallowed saliva and continued. He had never dared to say this to his daughter, but knew the time had come.

'Your mother didn't die of sorrow, she died of liver cancer… and she carried on drinking right until the end. She said it eased the pain.' He looked at his daughter and saw, grief-stricken, how Carmucha's sweet eyes, fixed insolently on him, suddenly filled with tears, tears of shame and fear.

'But… you said she was very sad because she couldn't go to school!' Her throat squeezed her voice, demanding a lament, and could barely emit the words.

'You weren't even fourteen. You were far too young to know the things of life, Carmucha.' Matías was dying to put an end to the confrontation that separated him from his daughter. 'I think the time has come to leave it,' he tried to take her hand to share these moments of agony, but she stood up, rejecting all contact. Matías felt as if a ship had left port, sounding its horn, just as he had arrived in an attempt to get on board.

'Not a word. It was my idea and I'm the one who decides when it's over.' Having stood up, Carmucha didn't know what to do. She didn't want to leave, but nor did she want to sit back down. Everything struck her as a form of fleeing.

'The guards respect you because I protect you. Were I to retreat, they could gun you down on any street corner.'

'Are you threatening me?' She had finally found an exit, someone she could blame for that pain that burned her chest. She gazed at her father defiantly.

'Don't talk rubbish, you know perfectly well I would give my life for you.'

Carmucha let out a guffaw laden with irony and spat on the floor, as if she was at Roxelio's, as if Matías had come out with such a great whopping lie it was almost funny. He couldn't bear to see her behave in this way and lost his temper. He banged the table so hard he almost broke a bone.

'You're as crazy as the rest of them. The money has made you all blind.'

Carmucha nodded.

'All except you, right, Papa?'

'The war will finish one day, and things will go back to the way they were before. Understand?' He stood up, resisting the desire to give her a beating. 'Don't count on me anymore. This business is over for me. I don't want to get my brains blown out because of your temerity.' Matías left the room, trying to repress his fury.

Carmucha placed her hands on the table, breathing quickly. She was overwhelmed by emotion. She ran to the cemetery and wept on her mother's grave in a way she had never wept before, letting all the anguish and all the hatred that consumed her insides come out. She apologized for being so stupid, for not understanding anything, for letting herself be carried along. She wept like a low tide, slowly, the waves breaking softly and silently, diminishing for hours.

It took her a while to find the house key among all the keys on the ring. She was anxious to talk to her father, to ask for forgiveness as she had done with her mother's memory at the cemetery. She opened the door and saw Milagros cleaning in the hallway. She asked after Matías and the maid said he had just left with a suitcase. She added the bit about the suitcase while staring at the floor, apparently confused, as if she'd been listening behind a door and knew all about Carmucha's argument with her father.

Carmucha thought her father had run away, but pretended everything was normal, hiding her concern behind a smile and an expression of thanks, as if there was nothing alarming or even strange about the fact he'd taken a suitcase. But as she headed to her room, she considered the possible consequences of that escape. She believed what he'd said might be true. His absence might signify the loss of the invisible shield that had been protecting her, preventing anybody from shooting her in the back of the neck when she was wandering about the red-light district on her own, preventing her from being gunned down on some track on the mountain. The revelation about the real cause of her mother's death had opened her eyes and made her re-examine everything from a new perspective. Emily's memory had become a little more human, weaknesses included, and this had enabled her to gain an awareness of her own vulnerability. She'd always looked at her mother as in a mirror, but the image she compared herself to was her mother's, and the more idealized it was, the less real was the other. She compared herself to a perfect heroine and what she saw reflected was something similar to a character from a comic who was capable of anything, invulnerable. But at that moment the mirror had smashed and what was left underneath was simply a woman. Carmucha carried on taking steps to enter the adult world, adding new data to the idealistic perception she'd conceived during her childhood. Before reaching her room, she heard the bell. She got to the door ahead of the maid and looked through the peephole. Colin was standing on the porch. He looked very spruced up, as if he wanted to appear formal. It amused her to see him like this. She remembered her eyes were red from crying, but didn't mind. She opened the door.

'Hello. What are you doing here?' she asked with a miner's brutality.

'Well… I thought you might like to go for a walk,' mumbled the Englishman, endeavouring to perform the role of a formal gentleman. 'Is your father at home?'

'A walk?' she replied, ignoring this reference to her father. Colin nodded, looking for something to do with his hands so he wouldn't appear nervous. 'It's just I don't normally go for walks with men. If you're seen with me, your reputation might suffer.'

Milagros, who was pretending to work without listening to the conversation, repressed a mischievous giggle and went to do something else so they could talk in peace.

'I don't have a very good reputation anyway, because I'm a foreigner. Most people think I'm shameless, that's why I wanted to talk to your father.'

Carmucha didn't want to explain what had happened. She felt trapped. She fancied going for a walk with Colin, relaxing and forgetting her anguish, but at that precise moment she didn't know how to do this.

'Excuse me, but…' she wasn't sure how to continue and simply closed the door. She did this slowly, as if hoping Colin would jump in without being invited. When the lock clicked, she waited on tenterhooks. Nothing could be heard on the porch, not even a footstep. She waited a little longer and opened again. Colin was still there like an English geranium. Carmucha's smile spoke volumes.

It was getting dark at Mar de Lira when they walked along a path that led from the main road to Carnota beach. In the background, the pink stone of Mt Pindus looked black, outlined against the purple sky. The waves of the low tide slowly and noisily repeated their cycle of explosions as they collided with the shore. Next to the path, Carmucha's vehicle watched, illuminating them with its headlights. The silhouette of a ship could be seen on the horizon; it was heading to Finisterre in order to turn south, in search of South America.

'Wouldn't you like to go back to your country on one of those ships you send there?' Colin was about to put an arm around her shoulder, but at that precise moment Carmucha happened to move forward to clear an obstacle from the path. Colin aborted his movement. 'Perhaps you'd prefer to go to New York, since you're always talking about *Manhattan Transfer*.' Carmucha turned to look at him. Colin, who still had his arm out in order to reach her, quickly pulled it back and put his hands in his pockets. 'Isn't it dangerous to send wolfram on a boat with all those German submarines?' she added.

Colin stared at the waves in order to gather strength and finally take her hand. But when he did this and felt the contact of her skin, his courage failed and, instead of coming out with a declaration, he started confessing all his secrets.

'The submarines are falling like nine pins, and the wolfram doesn't go to England. We throw it in the sea a few miles from here.'

'But... but then why...?' she said, instinctively letting go of Colin's hand.

They continued going down a track that led to the enormous half-moon-shaped beach. At the edge of the dunes, a group of seagulls was staring out to sea, watching the low-level flight of cormorants.

'To get it away from the Germans and make them pay a price that is unsustainable for their economy.' Colin took her hand again. They had reached the beach. They gazed at the seascape, which was extraordinary, but didn't see it. They only had eyes for each other.

'I never notice things,' she said with a childish grin. Colin, seeing she didn't let go of his hand, returned the smile, a smile that led to a kiss, a sweet kiss, a kiss of relief.

'The Germans will lose the war and soon everything we're doing at the moment will lose its meaning.' Colin was thinking about the future, afraid of being transferred just when he had found her.

'Nothing has meaning in this life,' said Carmucha, remembering her family tragedy. She then threw herself on his lips with all the fury she'd been holding inside, with all the passion she devoted to things that captured her attention.

The waves carried on beating close to the lovers' silhouettes, but the tide was turning. It was starting to come in, and the waves broke with increasing strength as the sun sank behind the horizon.

When the sun reappeared at the start of a new day, Félix arrived at the big house on horseback. Carmucha's car was parked at the entrance. There was a smattering of mist and the morning was colder than normal for this time of year. The horse was sweating. You only had to look at the animal to see they'd come in a hurry, but observing Félix's face you might also have deduced there was something wrong. He entered the house, blowing on his nails, and climbed to Carmucha's bedroom.

'Carmucha. Are you awake? The guards went to get Pepiño from his house. He only escaped by a miracle.' Without waiting for an answer, he opened the door and found Carmucha wasn't alone. The Englishman was in bed with her. They were awake, ashamed of being caught in flagrante, and sluggishly covered themselves with the sheets, not knowing how to react. Félix received a terrible blow. He had fleetingly pictured that vision the night he'd seen them together in the Casino, but when he saw it as a reality in front of his eyes, it was like attending the execution of his most intimate dreams, as if all the air had been sucked out of him. He closed the door again without saying anything and leaned against the wall, taking deep breaths to avoid fainting. He then heard the mattress creak and moved away down the landing with the intention of reaching the stairs, but Carmucha came out of her bedroom and called him. He stopped without turning around, thinking she was going to apologize because he thought he deserved an apology.

'I'm going to sort out things with Yellow once and for all, and I'd like you to come with me,' she said, ignoring the embarrassing situation that had just happened.

'Well, I'm going a-whoring in Noia, because it seems everybody here is fucking except me.'

Félix left without looking at her. Carmucha was stunned. She had never thought Félix might be attracted to her. They had spent so much time together since they were children that she viewed him like a brother, like a close friend with whom she had no secrets, but it had never occurred to her to think of him as a man or a possible lover. She'd always assumed he felt the same way, but at that precise moment she understood she had been totally mistaken in this as well.

She decided to go and sort things out with Yellow on her own. The meeting would take place far from the mine and the red-light district, in a house in the poor district on the outskirts of Noia. Carmucha climbed the stairs with fear thumping in her chest. She reached the top floor, where the attics were, and waited on the landing. These rooms were rented out for clandestine relationships away from prying eyes, in an isolated, discreet place.

A few minutes after her arrival, the door opened and Coñoño came out, naked from the waist up. The boy went to the communal toilet at the end of the landing and peed noisily. Carmucha came up and whispered to him.

'Are you sure you want to do this?'

Coñoño nodded with a serious gesture. He didn't look like the half-stupid boy she'd met a short while before. He exuded confidence. Carmucha handed him the hammer. The boy grabbed it with determination and headed back to the room. When he went in, he left the door open.

'Why have you left the door open?' asked Yellow bad-temperedly.

Carmucha saw through the opening how the guard, who was also naked from the waist up, sat up just in time to see the hammer flying towards him. He tried to dodge the blow, but the hammer grazed his face, making his ear bleed and crashing into his collarbone with the dull sound of broken bone. Yellow grimaced in pain. Coñoño was stunned. He seemed incapable of dealing another blow. Carmucha used this moment to enter the room, gripping a small axe. The guard understood he'd fallen into an ambush. He grabbed a knife he had on the bedside table and tried to stab her in the heart, but Carmucha jumped back and only received a small puncture in the ribs. Coñoño then found the strength to attack again, in an attempt to defend Carmucha, and dealt him another blow. This time, he hit him right in the middle of his yellow, shit-coloured head and Yellow fell at Carmucha's feet, the exact opposite of what had happened on the day they met. Carmucha didn't want to run any risks and without thinking, with unusual fury, she made sure she wouldn't have to deal with him again by hitting him repeatedly with the axe. She hit him so many times it was as if she wanted to obliterate him completely. Coñoño watched, open-mouthed, his chest covered in blood. When she finally stopped and saw the way the boy was looking at her, she understood the brutality of what she'd just done. Her enemy's inert body was a mass of gore.

Her breathing, instead of slowing down when she stopped, got faster and faster. She was about to succumb to panic, but managed to collect herself and take off her shirt, which was soaked in blood. She looked at her wound, which struck her as superficial. She cleaned it with the shirt. She then cleaned the blood that had splashed on Coñoño's chest, using the same blood-stained shirt. Impressed by what he'd just been through, Coñoño let her work as if he was a little child being seen to by his mother. Carmucha took out a large wad of notes and gave it to the boy.

'Tonight you have to catch the train to Barcelona, I've written down Rebeca's address. She'll help you find somewhere to live. OK?' The boy nodded, trembling with excitement. 'Come on, let's get out of here.'

The weather is very changeable in this land, even more changeable than people's moods. The sun which filled the room now hides in fear. Black clouds govern the world. The sky is about to collapse on top of our heads, broken into countless stones of ice.

The old man looks out of the window.

'How could she do that?' The girl is disappointed. It hurts her that Carmucha could do such a horrible thing.

'You know adolescence is a difficult time. Having suffered so much back then, she achieved everything in a very short time and ended up believing she really was the miners' queen.'

'Is that why she chopped him up with an axe?' says the girl with an expression of disgust.

'Monarchs are sometimes obliged to kill in defence of their people. The rage with which she did it was a result of the hatred she felt towards him, but she believed after that death there would be more justice on the mountain.'

'What nonsense, Grandpa. Who believes that kind of thing?'

'Remember the government was illegitimate. It had overthrown legally elected representatives. It had usurped power after a military rebellion and a war that took the lives of many thousands of people. Those were other times, Marica.'

'Well, I'm just glad we don't live in those times.' The girl puts her hand in a box of biscuits lying by the sofa, next to the remote control. She eats a couple. The old man sits down again. 'And so her father just ran away, without saying anything else?'

'She thought that, because she still believed he was selfish and cowardly. That was one of the main reasons she had to rebel. She was trying desperately not to be the way she thought her father was. That happens to lots of people, which is why fashions come and go in cycles.' The old man holds out his hand, asking for a biscuit.

'But there are also lots of people who only want to be like their parents. I have schoolmates who are repulsive. They dress like old people and go around, saying, "My father said this, my mother said that."' The girl hands him a biscuit.

'Yes, there are always rebellious and settled people. But almost everybody has mistaken ideas about the lives of adults.'

'Why do you say that? That's not true. Trouble is adults are repulsive.'

'Adults are children like you who just aren't so young anymore, Marica. They also did stupid things when they were a certain age, but if they made it to today, it's because they didn't do anything so stupid that it destroyed their lives, or because somebody saved them.'

'All right, Grandpa. Stop with all that nonsense and tell me what happened, you're starting to sound like my father.'

An insistent, repetitive sound invaded her nightmares. She opened her eyes. The room was barely illuminated by the glimmer of dawn. The sound could still be heard. It was as if someone was knocking at the door with their knuckles. Carmucha got out of bed, half dazed by sleep, and found she had succumbed to a fever. It wasn't a symbolic fever this time. It was a fever brought on by an infection. The wound Yellow had inflicted on her ribs was as real as the insistent beating she could hear. The wound was infected. She realized someone was knocking at the door of the house. She advanced down the hallway as if walking on a field covered in freshly mown grass. To begin with, she thought the ground was as soft as cake, but then realized she was dizzy. She opened the peephole and saw Félix, who carried on knocking, banging on the door with his fist. She opened the door.

Félix rushed in. His expression was a mixture of anger and fear.

'You really have lost your mind this time, haven't you?' Félix didn't notice her feverish state and sat on a bench in the hallway, panting out his nervous state. Carmucha closed the door and wiped the sweat off her temples. 'You kill somebody and then just fall asleep. You think you're so free you're going to end up in the clutches of that freedom.'

'I didn't kill…' Félix interrupted her, jumping to his feet. He grabbed hold of her shoulders, shaking her while talking in a fury.

'Listen, don't mess me about. Can't you see I've come from the red-light district, which is chock-a-block with policemen and everything?' Carmucha, pierced by the pain from her wound, realized this was not the time for pretences. She sat on the bench Félix had just vacated, grimacing as she felt another twinge. 'What's wrong with you, are you wounded?' The man softened his tone, fearing for her health.

'It's just a pinprick. What do they know?' she asked, giving the impression her appearance was more alarming than her condition.

'Not much, it seems, but they're questioning everybody. You should hide.' The information Félix gave her calmed Carmucha down. If they didn't know anything, it was because the plan had worked to perfection.

'Only one person could talk, and he's far away from here by now.'

'That's your business, I've warned you.' Félix made as if to leave, but Carmucha's pleading look held him back. He stopped before opening the door and spoke to her affectionately, 'Do you have a fever?'

Carmucha shrugged her shoulders. Félix's hand was on the door handle. He felt as if a magnet was pulling on his body, trying to take him far away from there, but he went up to her and put his hand on her forehead.

'You're boiling. Where's your Englishman?' He pronounced the word 'Englishman' with contempt, as if Colin was somehow to blame for what she'd done.

'He's away in Coruña because of a shipment.' Félix contorted his features. 'And my father has left the business and disappeared.'

Félix sighed awkwardly and sat down beside her. Carmucha, confused by the fever, didn't comprehend her real situation, she wasn't aware she had turned into an outcast. Nobody would want to be with a fugitive who was guilty of killing a civil guard.

'I have a daughter, you know? She's a year and a half...'

Now it was Carmucha who interrupted him.

'And the mother?'

'No, the mother left,' he said with a smile, trying to hide the shame he felt at the mother not being there to help him raise the child.

'But… why didn't you tell me?' Carmucha stared at him reprovingly.

'I don't know. Perhaps I thought if I told you, you might want to settle down… or make me settle down.' With these ambiguous words, Félix confessed he hadn't told her before because he'd been afraid of losing her. He confessed he'd always secretly thought about the possibility of their being together. By saying this, he also confessed the end of his hopes. Carmucha understood everything. She stroked him affectionately and gave him a fraternal look. She still loved him like a real brother.

'Go to her, why don't you?' she said from the heart.

Félix stood up, staring at her with anguish. Even though he was thinking about his daughter, it struck him as cowardly to abandon Carmucha. He opened the door to leave, but turned around at the last moment.

'Come on, grab some clothes, we're going to hide on the mountain.' Félix felt comforted when he saw the glint in Carmucha's eyes.

'First we have to go back to the women's school,' she said with an apologetic gesture.

'Are you crazy, or is that the fever attacking you?'

'I have to warn them,' she declared in her most stubborn voice. When she spoke like this, no force in nature was capable of holding her back. Félix sighed and helped her to her feet, knowing he wouldn't be able to convince her to escape without first giving that warning.

Félix parked Carmucha's car near the red-light district, and they walked from there. When they reached the women's school, Carmucha was sweating profusely because of the effort she'd made, in her feverish state, to walk without stumbling or attracting attention. No sooner had they entered than they realized they were too late. Everything was a mess. The furniture was upside down and had been smashed. Carmucha felt herself going weak at the knees. The twinges from the wound got stronger when she saw how her work had been destroyed. Félix insisted on leaving, thinking the people responsible for that destruction might still be in the house, but before he could convince her, he heard the sound of someone coming down the stairs. He hid and told Carmucha to run as soon as he jumped on top of whoever was coming down. But the footsteps belonged to the Ourensan, whose appearance was similar to that of the school. With swollen eyes, one sadly tinged blue, a broken nose and lips covered in dried blood, she looked like the instrument the policemen had used to smash up the premises. Carmucha wanted to ask her forgiveness for not arriving in time to warn her, but she replied it wasn't the first time she'd been 'interrogated' and made it perfectly clear only the police were to blame for their own brutality. She told them what she knew. A body had turned up – she didn't know whose it was – and the police wanted to know who was responsible. She thought they didn't have a clue who it was and that was why they were lashing out like this, but advised Carmucha to hide if she knew anything. She added it would be better not to tell anybody what she knew because people can't tell what they don't know.

When they went out into the street, they coincided with several officers who were looking for signs of suspicious activity. Carmucha had changed clothes with the Ourensan and, walking with her head on her companion's shoulder, didn't look so different from any other woman in the district. Félix supported her with his body. She had a bottle in her hand to hide the fact she couldn't walk properly, to give the impression it was because of her drunken state. They were about to reach the car when she almost fell over. Her knees buckled and Félix had to hold her up. An officer came around the corner just in time to view the scene. Félix stopped, took a swig from the bottle and, using the fact the policeman was walking right towards them, reprehended the girl for drinking more than she could handle. The policeman smelled the alcohol they had sprinkled on her clothes and swallowed the story whole. He even told them to move along. They reached the car and sped away.

Not long after that, the police arrived at the shack where Coñoño lived. They had received some information and thought this deviant, half-stupid boy might know something about an affair that was starting to seem as turbid as it was disagreeable. The shack was empty, but his few belongings were still there, as if the bird that nested there had escaped suddenly. They searched the plot, but could find no trace of him. They were just about to leave when one of them thought he saw something move behind a stack of branches heaped in the corner. They removed some of the branches and found Coñoño hunched against the wall, as defenceless as a bird that falls out of the nest before having enough plumage to fly. He was trembling with fear and crying in his hiding place, incapable of escaping or even moving.

That night, Félix watched over Carmucha as she slept. One moment, she sweated like a fountain; the next, she shivered with cold, wrapped in two blankets they had taken from the big house. They had sought refuge in the cave on the mountain, where the only help they had was the bow Carmucha had hidden in her childhood in case of emergency.

The moonlight filtered in through the gaps, painting patches of clarity on the girl's face. Félix spoke to her in a murmur, the way he did when his daughter was asleep in her crib, and confessed what he had never confessed before. His features withered by sadness, he told her all his secret adventures and related how with the earnings from the wolfram he had bought a bar in Coruña. It was looked after by a comrade-in-arms, whom he kept separate from his other affairs, in case things went pear-shaped one day and he had to disappear for a time. She slept an agitated, disturbed sleep. She gave a start, as if she could hear what Félix was saying, and uncovered herself when she turned inside the blankets. He covered her again with great affection and left with a shrunken heart. That was the last time he would ever see her.

Carmucha woke up shortly after dawn. She called for Félix without receiving an answer. She was still sweaty and feverish. She peeped outside. Then she understood she was alone with her fever and lay down in the cave again, covered in the blankets, trembling with cold and despair.

At that same moment, Milagros was opening the door of the house in Noia. Colin had come to ask after Carmucha and seemed anxious to learn something of her whereabouts. As soon as he heard about the death of the civil guard, he imagined she might be involved, despite the fact he knew nothing about the rape, though I can't be sure of that – with spies, who always speak to God and the Devil, who knows? He endeavoured to introduce himself, but the maid, who was as bright as a button, knew perfectly well who he was. She let him come in and call the big house on the phone. Mrs Manuela could only say Carmucha's car was in the shed, but had no news about Carmucha or her son. Colin had just hung up when Matías arrived. Milagros withdrew and left them alone.

They were talking for the first time and the situation between them was tense. For some time now, Matías had been aware of the interest Carmucha aroused in the Englishman, quite apart from purely commercial questions. But he'd always thought he was an adventurer who lacked formality and preferred to feign ignorance, waiting for all that to become part of history when the business with the wolfram came to an end. He was confident this relationship wouldn't leave a permanent trace. He was surprised to see him there, but seemed very pessimistic when Colin offered to help in any way he could.

'I tried to warn her, but made a mistake. I asked her to abandon that adventurous lifestyle, but she went and did the exact opposite,' complained Matías, lowering his head sorrowfully.

'Not everything is lost. We could try to get her out of the country.'

'The borders have been put on alert and so have the smugglers. Nobody would dare to help us.' He carried on shaking his head, feeling utterly discouraged.

'And the money?'

'We didn't earn that much. Carmucha didn't know this, but I spent a large part of it on commissions.'

'I can imagine, but I have wolfram.'

Matías finally raised his head. That magical word could do everything, even raise the spirits of a desperate man. He looked at him very seriously, disbelief on his face.

'Are you suggesting selling your wolfram to the Germans?' Colin nodded without blinking, without the slightest trace of doubt. 'That could cause you problems in the future.'

'I find it difficult to imagine a future without Carmucha.'

This response from the Englishman almost made him cry. He realized this man he'd thought was shameless was capable of risking his life to save his daughter.

'How much do you have?' he asked.

'Enough to solve many people's lives.'

'The people whose wills we have to buy have solved their lives already.'

'Even so…' said Colin calmly. 'We're talking about lots of money.'

Matías stood up and gave him a hug. Finally, he could see a ray of hope.

'Do you know where she's hiding?' he asked, pulling away from the embrace.

'No. The car is at the big house, but Mrs Manuela knows nothing about her.'

'Let's go then. I think I know where she might be,' he said, gesturing to him to follow.

Matías took Colin to the cave. He remembered perfectly well the day he'd taken Carmucha the first time and how much she'd liked it. The girl had turned that place into a private refuge and loved to go there to play like a new Robinson, lost in that infinite forest. When they entered the cavity, Carmucha was trembling like a branch on a windy day. Her face lit up when she saw them. Apart from being happy that she might now receive some help, she was far more relieved to understand she'd been mistaken when she thought her father wouldn't remember this hiding place from her childhood.

They took her back to Noia, hidden in a car Colin had borrowed, and put her in his house once night had fallen. Since they'd kept their relationship a secret, they thought the police wouldn't go looking for her there. Matías helped to put her to bed. Colin entered with a silver box that contained a hypodermic syringe and started preparing an injection. Carmucha, half dazed by the fever, thought he really was a doctor who had come to treat her, but Matías viewed him with distrust.

'It's called penicillin,' said Colin. 'It serves to cure infections.'

'I never heard of such a thing.'

'It's a new medicine. So far, only doctors in the allied army have it,' he said, shrugging his shoulders at Matías' surprise. 'My half brother is a military doctor in the British army.' He gestured to Matías. 'Help me with Carmucha.'

Her father hesitated, but seeing his daughter was sweating like a horse, he decided to remove the bedclothes. Colin gave her an injection, saying it would soon have an effect. It seems incredible to think there were no medicines for infections until those years, doesn't it?

Matías and Colin set to work in secret, with the aim of obtaining the money they needed to buy wills and try to save Carmucha. The Casino president acted as a cicerone to bring about an apparently accidental conversation between Colin and Don Rüdiger. They used a pause after the German's game to offer him the wolfram and try to agree a price. He found the offer so surprising, however, that he thought it was a trap. Colin had to convince him, saying he was fed up of watching money pass through his hands without closing his fist a single time to take a handful. He explained he'd decided to sort out his retirement before all this finished. Having transferred all that money, he knew all he'd get from the government was a kick that would land him in a sordid civil servant's job with a miserable salary. Don Rüdiger accepted these arguments and planned to do exactly the same as Colin when the moment arrived, so he ended up trusting him, understanding that the moment had already arrived. Naturally, he tried to make the best of the situation to lower the price as much as possible. People were paying four hundred pesetas a kilo, but with the excuse it was impossible to maintain such prices, he offered a measly two hundred, with the secret intention of recording in the books that he'd bought the wolfram at the current market rate.

Matías had withdrawn after the introductions and was watching from the bar. Seeing Colin sweat, he could imagine the difficulties he was going through. He kept rubbing his face, tapping his nose and grabbing his ear lobes. He did this to calm his nerves, but also to inform about the progress of the negotiations. They had agreed a set of signals to communicate the amount being offered by the German, so Matías could give his approval before Colin accepted the offer. Matías had the last word because he was the one who would have to buy off the influential people his daughter's destiny depended on. Having argued for a while, which seemed far too long to Matías, Colin touched his ear with two fingers and his nose with three. This meant the offer was two hundred and thirty. There didn't seem to be any way of getting more, but they had decided not to sell for less than two hundred and fifty. Colin looked beaten and crestfallen. He got up to leave, but the German stopped him, making one last offer. After this all-or-nothing stake, in which Colin threatened to offer the wolfram to a false Portuguese intermediary who would pay three hundred, he managed to get two hundred and fifty pesetas per kilo of wolfram.

Colin sat down while pretending to reflect and touched his nose with all his fingers, as if instinctively massaging it while he thought. Matías gestured his approval and saw Colin continuing with the negotiations to fix the date and place of delivery.

Carmucha was still hidden in the Englishman's house, but couldn't bear all this passivity. She was informed of what had happened and couldn't accept Coñoño being imprisoned because of her. Instead of lamenting the boy's inability, she cursed the idea of getting him involved in a war that didn't belong to him. Her blood was boiling after two days spent in bed. Suddenly the fever had disappeared because of the penicillin and she felt much better.

She jumped out of bed and got dressed. She was still weak and when she went out into the street, her legs were trembling. It was a lovely afternoon with people walking in the park. The girls carried on showing off their new dresses, while the boys watched with their noses pressed against the shop window. Carmucha saw their happy faces, oblivious to their destinies, and wished she could be like them, just another girl, a girl sauntering along until a boy arrived to lead her to the altar. She knew, however, that her life could never be so simple. She had lost that opportunity to live a monotonous, foreseeable life. She was overwhelmed by remorse. She couldn't get the image of the crushed, bloody body out of her mind. She thought she had to pay for what she'd done, she didn't deserve her father getting her out of trouble. However wretched shit-faced Yellow may have been, she had had no right to take his life. She reached the police station and went up to the policeman standing sentry on the door.

'A boy has been arrested for the murder of a civil guard, but I'm the one who's responsible,' she said to the officer's obvious surprise.

She spent several hours in a cell lit by a skylight. The cell smelled bad. It smelled of dampness and fear. It smelled of daily tragedy and sorrow. The walls were thick and, from the time they had put her in there, the world seemed to have fallen asleep.

All she could hear were muffled echoes of sentences she didn't understand, the footsteps of officers on duty or the odd siren that filtered through the openings when a factory shift ended or children came out of school. She then heard the sound of keys turning in the lock. She stood up. She thought she was finally going to be interrogated, but the person who came into her cell was her father. Carmucha jumped off the bed to give him a hug. Matías couldn't help remembering Carmucha running to throw her arms around his neck when he went to fetch her from school. He remembered the girl's face filling with happiness when she saw him, as if his arrival meant the revival of the entire world. Carmucha repeated the gesture, the smile. The hug immediately erased the tensions that had separated them for months.

'How are you?' asked Matías without pulling away from the embrace.

'I'm much better… it must be the medicine.'

'All the same, sit down. You must be very tired after all that fever.' Matías led her back to the bed and made her sit down. She let herself be led.

'I don't have fever anymore, Papa.' She spoke with the kind of affection she hadn't shown for some time and her father received this like a second hug. This sentence was almost an admittance of guilt. But he didn't blame her for anything.

'You shouldn't have handed yourself in. Colin and I are trying to sort this out.'

'I did it, Papa. And they're punishing someone else because of me.' The two of them sighed. 'I made a mistake and must pay the consequences.'

Matías grew emotional in front of her serenity.

'You've been paying ever since you were a child.' The two of them swallowed saliva. 'I'm going to get you out of here, you can be sure of that,' he said, trying to encourage both himself and her.

But it wasn't going to be easy. A veil of fear darkened his smile.

'Will you be able to forgive me one day, Papa?'

'Of course, my love. I can forgive you anything.'

He was finally able to smile sincerely. He had been wanting to say this for months, wanting to forgive his daughter, but until then hadn't known how to do it.

On 7 June 1944, Matías was doodling with a pencil on the front page of a newspaper placed on the desk in his office in the Casino. He was mechanically going over a drawing of France, tracing and retracing circles on Brest, Cherbourg and Dunkirk. Next to the map was a small photograph of parachutists beneath a sky dotted with planes. The headline talked about the first phase of the allied invasion directed by General Eisenhower. Another headline reported that the German command, fearing this was just a distracting manoeuvre, was waiting to learn the real centre of gravity of the attack so they could concentrate all their military might with the aim of repelling the attack.

As in Normandy, in that office there were two opponents. Severo was sitting opposite Matías, but despite his proximity, they were separated by an abyss. Even their usual camaraderie seemed to have grown cold suddenly. They had been talking for a while, but had fallen silent because of the impossibility of reaching an agreement.

'Somebody has to pay for this, Matías. You can't imagine the doors I've knocked on, and every time they send me further up.'

'Then let that poor wretch take responsibility for the death, and that's it.' Don Severo shook his head. 'How much does it cost to change a witness statement?' Matías broke the pencil with the impetus that forced him to keep fighting.

'It's not only that. Look at the papers, God damn it! Look how the war is going. And there are things people are saying that don't get published; I've heard all kinds of rumours. Politics is a mess and they want to set an example. It's not enough just to shoot a half-stupid homosexual.' Don Severo spoke vehemently because he was also having a bad time. He'd known Carmucha ever since she was a child and felt her father's suffering as his own. But he couldn't see an exit.

'What if I got hold of two million?' That was as far as Matías could go. If everything went perfectly, they might manage to amass such a fortune, but if the answer was still no, then he would have nothing more to offer.

Don Severo, who was staring at the floor, looked up with an expression of disbelief.

'Well, now, that's a lot of money. But even so, I'm not sure it will be enough.'

'I watched my wife die… I can't watch my daughter die as well. Do you understand?'

Don Severo found it hard to hold his friend's gaze. The situation and the options to solve it were difficult to bear.

It was dawn when six soldiers aimed their rifles at Coñoño's chest. The boy was blindfolded and sobbing. The bandage covering his eyes was soaked. The air was also very damp that morning. There was a mist.

There was a peal of thunder, but no storm. The lightning caused a red waterfall that emerged from his chest, splashing the ground with sinister drops. The lifeless body fell on top of them. Some drops of blood also spattered the wall where death had been waiting and slid slowly down until joining the others. It was all over now, but the blood spilt in vain seemed still to be looking for something. Perhaps it was seeking justice; perhaps it was just after the promise of a supernatural future, although poor Coñoño, dumb as he was and everything, didn't trust the priests.

Carmucha was still alone in her cell. She had a strange sensation of emptiness, solitude. It was as if a presentiment had flown through the mist to remind her of the presence of death.

She again heard the sound of the lock. The door opened. Matías smiled from the threshold.

Colin was waiting in front of the police station with a rented car. He saw Matías come out, accompanied by Carmucha. They were talking.

'This very morning you will leave for America on the *Magallanes*.' Matías had waited until they had left the station to talk to her, so nobody would hear what they were saying.

'What about Coñoño?' asked Carmucha in concern.

'He's been moved to Barcelona. They'll let him go in a couple of months.'

Carmucha scrutinized her father's face in search of some weakness, but couldn't discern the slightest trace of a lie. They were getting near the car – near Colin, therefore. Carmucha ran into his arms. Matías allowed them only a few seconds to embrace before opening the door and telling them to get in. He wanted to get out of there as soon as possible.

Carmucha was happy with her two men, sitting in the back of the vehicle. She held her father's hand, as if he was her boyfriend. She had realized how wrong she had been about Matías and felt ashamed of having distrusted him. That bad period, however, was behind them because her father had made it very clear she was forgiven. She planned to go to New York with Colin. She also had read *Manhattan Transfer*, the book he talked about so much. She tried to imagine that vertical world full of ants from every continent fighting to get ahead and was afraid, but after everything she'd been through in the last few days, she also felt a huge sense of relief. It was as if she was walking on the surface of the moon and her body was as light as a feather. She looked at Colin, who gave her a smile that didn't seem entirely full. She recalled she wouldn't see her mother's grave for a long time. This saddened her, but she hoped Matías would go in her place, at least until he finished the paperwork he needed to do to liquidate his fortune. She looked at her father, who was staring out of the car window, watching the fields rush past, as if trying to go back in time to remember the happy years of his youth.

Behind their vehicle was another with five men inside. They reached Vigo and headed straight to the port. The two vehicles passed between sheds, driving noisily over the irregular cobbles covered in putrid remains. They opened the doors and got out of the vehicle. The other car stopped behind them. Matías saw Carmucha viewing it with distrust.

'So, we have an escort. Come on, you, get your luggage,' he said to his daughter in a festive tone. He went to the other vehicle to greet Don Severo, who was travelling with an officer and three guards. The mayor was serious, he even looked ashamed. Matías shook his hand and patted him on the shoulder. The officer watched with a clearly hostile expression while the guards remained in the background.

'You've no idea how hard Severo had to work to reach this solution,' said Matías. Carmucha nodded with a timid gesture of thanks, but didn't know what to say. Severo endeavoured to smile, but could only stare at the ground. Matías anticipated his daughter's doubts and went over to her. He gave her a kiss. 'Right, we're staying here.' Then he spoke to Colin. 'Take care of her until we see each other again.' And he gave him a wink full of camaraderie.

'I will,' replied Colin, taking Carmucha's hand as she took a step towards her father.

'Come soon,' she expressed her desire as if it was a plea.

'Very soon.'

Carmucha swallowed when she saw her father surrounded by civil guards, but accepted the little tug Colin gave for them to leave.

Matías, Don Severo and the guards watched in silence.

Colin and Carmucha, weighed down with suitcases, started moving off, their eyes on the horizon. The sun was beginning to break through the mist, which hung in tatters off the masts of the ships. The port workers bustled about with the same vitality as the inhabitants of *Manhattan Transfer*. Carmucha looked back and saw her father waving, but when she saw Colin keep moving, staring in front as if something prevented him from turning his head, she stopped.

'Papa! Come with us now!' she shouted.

'I can't, Carmucha. When the time comes, I want to be able to rest next to your mother and there are a few papers I have to sort out.'

Everybody fell silent for a moment. Looks were exchanged, causing doubts to take up residence in their hearts.

'You'll have time for that later. I'd much prefer it if we left together!' Carmucha's voice had lost the confidence it normally exuded.

Matías moved forward, ready to give his daughter one final push, but the guards quickly grabbed him to prevent this.

'Leave him!' exploded the mayor, full of indignation.

The officer nodded silently and the guards let go of Matías.

Carmucha finally understood what was going on. Colin had his arm around her, but she pulled away and ran to embrace her father. In that final hug, they tried to recover all their lost embraces. Carmucha wept like a little girl. Matías was consoled, thinking, even if it was at the very last moment, he had regained her once and for all.

'Papa, I always thought…'

But she couldn't keep going because Matías' fingers gently covered her mouth. Her father shook his head so she wouldn't continue. He must have thought if he let her talk, he would end up collapsing and he wanted to take his leave while keeping his dignity, so she would preserve the memory of a man who was prepared to confront what awaited him.

'Your mother always said you have to lose lots of battles to win the war.'

'I just wanted…'

'You wanted to be a woman.' He fell silent, gazing at her with satisfaction. 'And you will be, my love.'

Carmucha threw herself at his breast, clinging to him desperately.

'You have to go now, before they change their minds,' he gave her one last kiss and moved in the direction of the guards – his executioners.

'We have to go now, Carmucha,' said Colin, but she tried to go back to her father. This time, the Englishman took a firm hold of her. Carmucha shouted, saying it was her, she was the guilty one, they had to release her father, they could go to hell. She shouted in despair until she felt her knees buckling and lost consciousness, slipping into darkness, as on the day she met Yellow.

The girl is silent. She wasn't expecting such a sad ending.

'Come on, you, take your jacket, it looks cold out. They'll be waiting.'

The old man heads towards the door, followed by the girl.

They go downstairs in silence.

This spring is crazy. The sun has dominion of the sky again. The two of them walk along the wet pavement.

'How come you know so many details of the story, Grandpa?'

'I saw some of them myself, others were told to me, while others I imagined over the course of the years, after thinking about them so much.' The old man walks nimbly, more nimbly than you would expect from a man in his eighties.

'But that means...' The girl doesn't dare continue; when she sees her grandfather's mischievous expression, however, she understands he knows very well what she's thinking. She is speechless with surprise.

'It was during the war. The sergeant said Valentín was no name for a soldier. So he called me Félix. Everybody called me Félix during the war. I liked it. Up in the mountains, my neighbours began to call me that. Until I had to disappear. Having left Carmucha in the cave, I escaped to Portugal until I could come back and reclaim the bar.' The old man points at the bar they're heading towards. Above the door is a sign that says 'Bar Valentín'. The girl looks at him as if she's seeing him for the first time.

'I can't imagine you could be so brutal or rather such a troublemaker, yes, troublemaker is the word.' The old man smiles with satisfaction. They're very close to the bar. The girl stops. 'What happened to Carmucha? Didn't you ever try to find out?'

'I think she arrived in New York and spent her life with the Englishman, but I never had contact with her after that. She may have grandchildren your own age.' Inside the bar, a man gestures to them to get inside. It's late. A woman serves food at a table.

'So Aunt Carme is that child?'

'Of course, that's why she's fourteen years older than your father.' The old man doesn't want to give any further explanations. He's been talking the whole morning. He thinks it's time for the girl now to turn things over in her mind and enters the bar to cut off the conversation. The girl follows him inside. She hears her father complaining that they're late. She's always late and her father always says she doesn't have a brain, she's always distracted because she's always thinking about stupid things. Then they argue and the two of them end up shouting. Today she starts by complaining it's not her fault they're late, but soon forgets that and gets into a fight in which her only concern is to be right, whatever her father might say. His only concern is to demonstrate she doesn't know everything, whatever she might say. In the end, her mother intervenes and the two of them sit down to eat with bad tempers. That said, the girl doesn't help to set the table as she's been asked. Her mother doesn't approve of this behaviour, she says she's always in a bad mood for no reason and asks what the hell is the matter. The girl exchanges a look with the old man, who answers for her.

'Kids' stuff,' he says, winking at the girl.

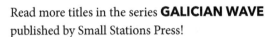

Read more titles in the series **GALICIAN WAVE**
published by Small Stations Press!

Marcos Calveiro, THE PAINTER WITH THE HAT
OF MALLOWS

A teenage boy is sent by his mother to spend a few days in the
country as a way of getting him out of trouble. In the town of
Auvers-sur-Oise, one hour north of Paris, the boy finds life with
his great-aunt unbearable – that is until the arrival of the painter Vincent van
Gogh, who has come to escape difficulties in the south. It is the summer of
1890 and already eight months have passed since the boy left his mother. He
begins a friendship with the painter, taking him to places he hasn't seen and
engaging in conversations that open his eyes to a different way of viewing
the world, bringing to an end his turbulent past. He also struggles with the
reasons for his mother's disappearance from the town where she grew up and
experiences the first embers of romantic love when he develops an interest
in the daughter of van Gogh's innkeeper, Adeline. Based on real events, this
imaginative story of a teenage boy's friendship with an inspired painter and
participation in the events of a provincial town, where he meets the local
doctor, a war hero, and railway pointsman, as well as the man who could turn
out to be his real father, rushes to its inevitable conclusion like the trains that
slice through the countryside on their way to Paris.

ISBN 978-954-384-030-4

Manuel Lourenzo González, BROTHER OF THE WIND

Khaled is an Iraqi boy, a member of the Koblai tribe, growing up in the village of Qhissa Hanni in the mountains of north Iraq. He has left school to look after his family's flock of sheep, but his father and the local schoolteacher think he has the makings of a writer, so they give him a notebook in which he records his aspirations, events in the village, the life of his family, his wish to own a horse which he will call 'Ahu al-Rih' or 'Brother of the Wind', his secret engagement to the mayor's daughter, Amrah, so secret that even she doesn't know about it, the time when he and a friend go frog hunting and slip a couple of frogs into the midwife's bag, causing havoc when the midwife is due to assist in the birth of Ilaisha's son… The book is presented as a series of letters which Khaled writes to the son of a European archaeologist, Dr Meira, nicknamed 'Al-Galego', who has taken up residence in the village in order to pursue his archaeological studies and because he has grown fond of the Iraqi way of life. But the invasion of the country in 2003 by the United States and its allies casts a heavy shadow over this remote village and its inhabitants, who struggle to come to terms with the issues that are at stake and who will have to draw on all their reserves of courage and strength if they are to survive. The war will bring tragedy to the village and will force Khaled to undertake a journey he has never imagined before, to the heart of the country's capital, Baghdad. This is a journey of principle, of courage over fear, of faith and friendship, of self-sacrifice, that will change Khaled's expectations forever.

ISBN 978-954-384-074-8

Antonio Manuel Fraga, TARTARUS

When Guiomar Brelivete, a thirteen-year-old schoolgirl who lives in Audierna, is told by her parents that she must start attending klavia lessons in the old quarter of Plugufan and miss training sessions for maila, her favourite sport, she is understandably annoyed. But her teacher, Mastrina Xaoven, turns out to have a sense of humour and agrees, in return for Guiomar learning to play the instrument, to tell her a story about a girl called Attica who is a member of the politically powerful Gwende community. The traditional inhabitants of the land, the Malluma community, have been confined to the nabrallos or suburbs, where Gwendes are not supposed to go. But one evening Attica boards a train to the nabrallo of Bragunde, hoping to attend a concert in one of the famous hicupé clubs, and there she meets Fuco, a Malluma boy who claims to be a firewalker. The nabrallo has been overrun by a plague of scorpions, and the children resolve to consult the witch Onga, Queen of the Cemetery, about this. They will learn that a far greater evil lurks beneath them, in the lost underground world of Nigrofe, where the balance between good and evil has been obliterated by the removal of a sacred tree, and it rests on them to restore that balance if only they can find a way in... In these two tales, the line between fiction and reality is blurred, and there is a striking resemblance between the old music teacher and the intrepid girl in her story.

ISBN 978-954-384-091-5

Read more Galician literature in English published
by Small Stations Press!

FICTION:

Fran Alonso, NOBODY
Anxo Angueira, LISTING SHIP
Xurxo Borrazás, VICIOUS
Marica Campo, MEMOIR FOR XOANA
Carlos Casares, HIS EXCELLENCY
Ledicia Costas, AN ANIMAL CALLED MIST
Álvaro Cunqueiro, FOLKS FROM HERE AND THERE
Xabier P. DoCampo, THE BOOK OF IMAGINARY JOURNEYS
Xabier P. DoCampo, WHEN THERE'S A KNOCK ON THE DOOR AT NIGHT
Pedro Feijoo, WITHOUT MERCY
Miguel Anxo Fernández, A NICHE FOR MARILYN
Miguel Anxo Fernández, GREEDY FLAMES
Agustín Fernández Paz, NOTHING REALLY MATTERS IN LIFE MORE THAN
LOVE
Paco Martín, THE THINGS OF RAMÓN LAMOTE
Teresa Moure, BLACK NIGHTSHADE
Teresa Moure, THE OPERATION
Miguel-Anxo Murado, ASH WEDNESDAY
Miguel-Anxo Murado, SOUNDCHECK: TALES FROM THE BALKAN
CONFLICT
Xosé Neira Vilas, MEMOIRS OF A VILLAGE BOY
Xavier Queipo, KITE
Manuel Rivas, ONE MILLION COWS
Manuel Rivas, THE POTATO EATERS
Susana Sanches Arins, AND THEY SAY
Anxos Sumai, HARVEST MOON
Anxos Sumai, THAT'S HOW WHALES ARE BORN
Suso de Toro, POLAROID

Suso de Toro, TICK-TOCK
Xelís de Toro, FERAL RIVER

POETRY:

Rosalía de Castro, GALICIAN SONGS
Rosalía de Castro, NEW LEAVES
Xosé María Díaz Castro, HALOS
Celso Emilio Ferreiro, LONG NIGHT OF STONE
Pilar Pallarés, A LEOPARD AM I
Pilar Pallarés, FOSSIL TIME & BOOK OF DEVORATIONS
Lois Pereiro, COLLECTED POEMS
Luz Pozo Garza, ONE CAMELLIA BLOSSOM: POETRY ANTHOLOGY
Manuel Rivas, FROM UNKNOWN TO UNKNOWN
Martín Veiga, JEWELS IN THE MUD: SELECTED POEMS 1990-2020

For an up-to-date list of our publications, please visit
www.smallstations.com